Sandy Mason

Cuban Exile

A Johnny Donohue Adventure

Sandy Mason

Cuban Exile

A Johnny Donohue Adventure

ISBN-13: 978-1533059949
ISBN-10: 1533059942

Contact Sandy …
SandyMason2782@aol.com
www.SandyMason.com
https://www.amazon.com/author/sandymason

Cuban Exile

For Jack Kennedy - Who Left Us Too Soon

Sandy Mason

For Soviet Naval Officer

Vasili Alexandrovich Arkhipov

Василий Александрович Архипов

January 1926 – August 1998

Who May Have Saved The World

"A man does what he must—
in spite of personal consequences,
in spite of obstacles and dangers and
pressures—and that is the basis of
all human morality."

Jack Kennedy – Profiles In Courage
1956

Sandy Mason

Bradenton Florida March 2010

Chapter 1

One of the more interesting characters who kept a boat at *Dolphin Cove Marina* in Bradenton, Florida was my friend, Dr. Sam Feldman. Sam is a dermatologist who owns a brand new Catalina Thirty-Eight sailboat aptly named *Epithelia*. Epithelia cells make up the outer surface of our skin – the surface upon which dermatologists focus a lot of their attention.

The boat was beautiful but Sam was too busy to ever use her. In fact, he didn't know enough to ever use her. That's where Lonnie and I come in to play. We are Sam's maritime support structure. We handle the sailing end of things … you know, mainsail, jib, electronics, navigation – all the minor stuff. This allowed Sam to be the pretend captain. He mostly liked to sit on the stern rail seats with their custom fitted cushions and tell stories.

Occasionally, when he brought a new female guest on board, we would coax him into saying something nautical such as 'Green buoy three, two o'clock." Whenever we approached an inlet, he would say out loud, "Remember guys, red, right, return."

These highly complex warnings made Sam sound like an expert, so they served their purpose. My personal favorite featured pulling into a slip. A while ago I taught him to yell out, "Grab the windward spring lines first guys." Although I'm quite sure he didn't know a spring line from an autumn moon, I told him that this single command elevated him to the status of coxswain aboard ship. Sam took full advantage of that position. His girlfriends often gave him a glowing smile as we eased into the slip. Officially, a coxswain is actually the helmsman or some other crew member in command of the vessel at a given time. Coxswain, I think, is the perfect title for Sam.

Epithelia had every single piece of optional equipment available and then some. It was fitted with the latest in marine electronics including state of the art navigation equipment.

There were display screens mounted on the binnacle as well as a full compliment of screens down below at the navigation station. There was a thirty-six inch flat-panel television mounted on the bulkhead and of course individual televisions in both the Captain's and the crew's quarters. A satellite dish mounted inconspicuously on the stern railing linked us up there into TV-land.

Being a skin doctor in Florida is like owning your own personal gold mine. Whenever you needed money, you just went out to your gold mine and loaded up with cash. The sun broiled everyone up, down and sideways. Then the skin guys removed spots, growths, bumps and whatever else they could cut away.

Of late though, Sam had been specializing in burn victims. In fact, he had become a leading expert in burn victim surgery and post-operative treatment. He is meticulous and precise in his surgery and careful to a fault. If I ever have burn surgery, I would want Sam to be the surgeon. What he lacked in sailing skills, he more than made up for behind the surgical mask.

Some people found Sam to be a pain in the ass but I found him to be intelligent, funny and quite engaging. I always had the feeling that Sam was purposely covering up his intelligence with laughter and the appearance of naiveté. The word around the marina was that he was a top surgeon in his chosen field of dermatology. There are many sides to Sam.

He had a rather amusing on-again, off-again, girlfriend who often was at his side. Her name was DeeDee. They were perfect together as neither one had a clue about how to run a sailboat. But I liked them both and we had many cocktails on *Epithelia* swapping stories in between hors d'oeuvres. Sam, Lonnie and I had been friends for a few years. DeeDee, I thought, was a somewhat whimsical addition to our little group and, let's face it; she had a figure that was easy to look at.

On this particular evening, the four of us sat in the cockpit. Sam threw us a curve ball when he asked Lonnie and me if we would sail with him and DeeDee to Key West. On the way he would give DeeDee some sailing lessons. I looked up at the sky and thought *that ought to be interesting.* I said. "Sam, Key West is not like going out for a day sail. You're talking about one hundred eighty miles or so! It takes a couple of days to get down there. Not to mention another couple of days to get back, plus some layover time. You're talking about a week or so."

Lonnie said. "What about your medical practice?"

"Well, I have that covered. I can manage my way around a week's worth of appointments. I've thought about this for awhile. I mean, what do I have this boat for anyway?"

I stared off into space looking for an answer to Sam's question. I do a lot of staring. "Well," I said, "The boat is certainly capable and you'd have ample time to show Miss DeeDee around the steering wheel." I was not ready to commit to a trip to Key West but I was giving it some thought. I could see Lonnie thinking it over as well.

We all kicked around thoughts of scheduling, work obligations, personal obligations and all the stuff you think about when you are about to disrupt your life's routine. Lonnie and I started talking about things that needed to be done to the boat to accommodate a trip to the Keys. After a couple of Heinekens, no issue seemed to be a show stopper. So, we agreed.

***

A week later we were provisioning the boat for a four person round trip to Key West. I left a float plan with some boat neighbors and another at the marina office. When Sam arrived at dockside, Lonnie told him to go over to the ship's store and get whatever he and his tootsie would want on a two day sail. By the look on his face, I think he expected me to do this. When we had finished loading up the boat, Lonnie and I went over our float plan with Sam as well as some details about the safety equipment. He paid close attention. Sam may have been inexperienced but he was not stupid.

Cuban Exile

A short time later, Miss DeeDee walked down the pier towards *Epithelia*. DeeDee and the doctor were somewhat comical to look at as a couple. Sam barely cracked five foot seven inches tall while DeeDee wore stiletto heels that made her hit six feet easily. She just didn't get the whole boat shoe thing. In fact, she just didn't get the whole boating attire thing. Today she had on a short red leather skirt with a white long-sleeve shirt that had been tied up at mid-naval area. Lonnie gave her a look while Sam smiled … a big beaming smile. I couldn't believe we were headed out to sea with this chick! It was definitely time for drink.

Our plan was to stay aboard *Epithelia* in our home marina that night and head out, not too early, the next day. First stop, *Venice Yacht Club*, Venice, Florida, about thirty or so nautical miles away, a trip of about six or seven hours.

Lonnie helped DeeDee aboard and diplomatically suggested that she go barefoot for the sailing trip. This idea was well accepted and off came the shoes. Sam took DeeDee below and showed her where their bunk would be. She seemed most interested in the head and the shower. Sam took her through the details of that for the ninth or tenth time as she put a huge cosmetic bag in the middle of the cabin deck area.

Lonnie went below and mixed drinks for everyone and carried them up to the cockpit on a tray. The four of us sat topside and talked about sailing, weather, safety equipment and supplies. DeeDee asked about restaurants along the way. Sam replied, "There's a restaurant at *Venice Yacht Club*, otherwise we can make dinner on board."

"Really," said an astonished DeeDee. "You can cook on this boat?"

You never knew whether she was being sincere or just pulling our chain. Lonnie could not resist. "Yeah, maybe you noticed the galley down below on the starboard side? You know, right by the bag that you put in the middle of the cabin?"

"Huh?"

"The galley is the boat kitchen, Honey, "Sam said. That seemed to end the conversation about meals, at least for awhile anyway. This was either going to be a fun trip or a disaster at sea. "Okay," DeeDee said, "I volunteer to help cook." Life is just full of surprises.

Chapter 2

The next morning we were preparing to leave the dock in Bradenton. We were shooting for an 8 AM departure. Lonnie, Sam and I were ready to go by 8 AM but DeeDee had trouble operating the marine head and the accompanying shower attachment. Sam had gone off to the ship's store and Lonnie was a few slips away - helping someone with sails.

That's when I heard some shrill girly screams coming from below. I went down the companionway steps and found the deck covered in three inches of water. It seems that DeeDee had mastered the art of turning on the shower head but had not yet mastered the art of turning off the shower head!

The automatic bilge pumps activated as the water from the shower was being vacated from the cabin out to a through-hull plug and into the river. I pulled open the door to the shower. Water came rushing out. DeeDee screamed and fell into my arms. I'm not sure if she screamed because she was stark naked or because water came pouring out of the shower stall and was now flooding the cabin! At any rate, I pulled her towards me as I reached up and around her in order to turn off the water intake valve.

I looked at her and couldn't help but smile. She was stark naked. Well, of course she was stark naked, she was taking a shower, for God's sake. I tried to ignore that fact, as much as one can ignore a beautiful naked woman in a shower.

We stood there for a few seconds looking at each other. Both of us were soaked. The shower was draining. The bilge pumps were pumping and the birds up topside were squawking loudly.

We started laughing – big ridiculous laughs – hard laughs. She reached for some towels to cover up with but they were soaked. We laughed some more. I found some dry towels in a locker and wrapped her up in one.

The laughs turned in to smiles. I helped her dry off and she gave me a kiss that turned out to be longer than I expected. I pointed her back to her cabin and then disappeared into my quarters to put on some dry clothes.

Lonnie returned just as I climbed up into the cockpit. He heard the noise from the bilge pump. "What's goin on down there?"

"Oh nothing, just checking out the pump. I spilled some water on the deck below to test something. Everything is fine."

He grunted a Lonnie grunt.

From that moment on I decided that I liked DeeDee. Okay, she was a little ditzy – maybe a lot ditzy - but she was fun and after the shower disaster began to show a genuine interest in the boat. Lonnie and I took turns answering some of her questions.

She had changed into blue jeans and a red sweatshirt with a matching cap. Now that was more like it. Sam returned from the ship's store just as the bilge pump shut off. We were finally ready to go.

I started the engine. Lonnie signaled me that the lines were clear so I put *Epithelia* into reverse and backed her out of the slip. We motored down the

Manatee River and headed toward the big range marker that pointed our way past Egmont Key and out into the Gulf of Mexico.

We sailed south and were happily pushed along by a cooperative and soothing east wind. Lonnie raised the main sail while I steered along the coastline towards Venice. DeeDee turned around and smiled at me. I thought about her naked in the shower, but quickly dispelled that thought.

I set the automatic pilot to the course that I needed and settled into a nap position. I drifted off while listening to Sam talk to DeeDee about some of the fine points of sailing. If he only knew what fine points I had already found.

Chapter 3

The dock boy at *Venice Yacht Club* helped us tie the boat up in a transient slip about 6 PM that evening. As far as I could tell, DeeDee thoroughly enjoyed the trip. Either she was a really good actress and faked being genuinely interested in boating or *she was* genuinely interested in boating. Who knew? Sam, on the other hand, was totally into the sail trip down from Bradenton. After some coaching, he took the wheel, checked our position and did all the stuff you're supposed to do when you are the helmsman. The way he went on, you would think he just sailed up from the South Pole.

We decided to have dinner on board the boat. DeeDee asked Lonnie to pull out some small plates that she planned on using to serve hors d'oeuvres. Lonnie put together drinks for everyone while I was topside giving Sam some detail about the sail configuration. He was enthusiastic and curious. He had owned his boat for a few years but had never gone more than five miles from the marina.

Today, he was oozing confidence and bursting with pride over his new found sailing skills. Over boat drinks he calculated our distance to Fort Myers. He forced our attention, including that of Miss DeeDee, in to listening to a basic nautical lesson. "You see, Dee, first you look at the map and find the approximate latitude and longitude of Fort Myers."

"The what?"

"The position, Sweetie."

"Oh yeah, the position."

"See, it's right here, twenty-six degrees, twenty-seven minutes north latitude. Then you just subtract the latitude of Fort Myers from our latitude here in Venice, that is twenty-seven degrees, six minutes. Then just calculate the difference in minutes and you have the north-south distance to our next destination. See, right here." Sam pointed to the chart. "There's about forty minutes of latitude between us, so it's about forty nautical miles. Oh, I forgot to tell you about nautical miles."

I broke in. "That's okay Sam, I'll explain it later."

DeeDee commented, "Wow, very cool Sam. I am going to fix dinner."

Off she went to explore the galley and put together her first meal at sea ... well, her first meal at the marina anyway. It occurred to me that she might not really cook anywhere - but I threw caution to the wind and awaited the result of this culinary adventure.

This was the perfect interlude to go up to the locker room to shower and put on a fresh outfit. I changed into jeans, a light blue collared shirt and a navy blue sailing jacket before heading for the bar at the yacht club.

I stood in the entranceway and looked into the cocktail lounge. Sam was inside, perched on a barstool. With the aid of a full portion of Chivas Regal, he was telling anyone who would listen how to navigate a thirty-eight foot sailboat. The bartender was a polite young lady who pretended to listen. Sam went on, "Yeah, then you have to be careful because there's regular miles and there's nautical miles. You can't mix 'em up."

This was my cue to enter the stage. I sat down on a stool next to Sam. "So, how are you, Doc?"

"Great, me and the guys over there have been talking about, you know, navigation and stuff."

"Oh yeah, were they receptive to you?"

"Sure, I told 'em we just sailed in from Bradenton. It was a rough trip but we made it in one piece."

"Look Sam, most of these guys could navigate rings around you."

The moment I said that, I felt bad. I didn't have to burst his balloon so abruptly. I should have left him to have his fun but instead I insisted he come back on board.

Sometimes I can get really impatient. It's one of the few bad character traits that I have. We both waved to the guys at the bar and walked down the pier headed for *Epithelia*. Sam spoke, "There's a lot to sailing, isn't there, Johnny? I don't just mean navigating and steering. You seem to be deeper into it, a part it. You have a feel for it and it has a feel for you. You're a rich man, Johnny. I'll never learn what you have learned from sailing but this trip will be great for me."

That was one of the nicest compliments I have ever received. Inside of himself, Sam was sensitive and caring. That fact just didn't surface as often as it should. I took the compliment and held it within my thoughts. I just said, "Thanks."

When we got back to the boat, we found the table below set for dinner. DeeDee had put together a simple dinner of salmon with wild rice and a side of broccoli. Lonnie opened a bottle of white and all was well aboard the good ship *Epithelia.* We stayed up way too late before closing down the boat and settling in for the night.

Chapter 4

The next morning began with Sam's cell phone ringing like there was no tomorrow. It sat on the table in the main cabin and blared away. The vibrate button was activated so the phone did kind of a dance on the table. The powerful ring easily awoke Lonnie and me. I went into that partial sleep, partial dream, and partial awake sequence as I stumbled out of my bunk. I reached over to the table in the main cabin and picked up the phone.

By the time I got to the phone, it had stopped ringing but the letters *TGH* were flashing on the screen. "What the hell was that?" said Lonnie.

"I don't know, but somebody named TGH wants to find Sam pretty bad."

"TGH is *Tampa General Hospital*, Genius. Go and roust Sam out of his quarters. There could be an emergency at the hospital."

As it turned out, this was the second time in two days that I found DeeDee naked in my arms. I had awoken her, and she sat straight up and looked at me for a few seconds. She had nothing on at all. Her skin looked pink in the moonlight as it danced through the portal and landed on that beautiful face. I looked at her as she pulled me to her chest and gave me a hug. It was the kind of hug that had the trappings of a casual middle of the night visit.

I smiled at her. "DeeDee, wake Sam up, we think there's an emergency of some sort." She was now perched on her knees leaning forward so her head did not hit the bulkhead … tits pointing right at me. "Huh?", she said.

"Wake up Sam. His phone is ringing " I said. I glanced at the little clock on the shelf in the master's quarters. It was 4:27 AM. DeeDee managed to wake Sam up and he came out of his quarters – naked – groggy – and a little bit hung over.

He returned the call to TGH and listened with great disappointment to the voice on the other end of the line. I sensed with my uncanny intuition that this was the last of my DeeDee showings.

There was a fire in Tampa that affected about twelve people - most with serious burn damage. Some victims required surgery. Sam got dressed in a hurry and unfortunately so did DeeDee. Sam called for a taxi as they packed up and prepared for a rapid departure to Tampa. The sailing trip of Sam's life had just taken a very wrong turn.

***

Lonnie and I stood in the cabin as if we were both hit by stun guns. It was just past 5 AM. The birds were not yet up. The dock lights were lit up like a runway. A ten-knot breeze kept the flag busy as some early morning fishermen made their way out into the Gulf of Mexico.

I put up some coffee. Lonnie used a semi-sarcastic and aggravated tone. "Okay, so what now, Genius?"

"Well, we were on our way to Key West, right? Carla has a slip reserved for us, right? So let's head to Key West."

Lonnie grunted. I continued, "It's not like Sam is going to use his boat or anything of that sort. If he wants to tell stories, and he will, he can tell them on our boat back in Bradenton."

I sat back and thought about things, not necessarily related to our current situation. For an adult male, I don't have many strings tying me down. I am single and live aboard my boat in Bradenton. Home is a thirty-four foot Mainship trawler named *LifeLine*. By now, I've been here in Florida for six or seven years.

Back then, I needed a change in lifestyle so I settled into beautiful *Dolphin Cove* – a full service marina on the Manatee River on Florida's west coast.

It was a big change from my life in New York City and it turned out to be a positive one. I think. I run a small software company that caters to marinas. This I do with my partner, Ed Dowd. I run my company at the navigation station in the main cabin of the *LifeLine*. I have a laptop, a cell phone, wireless internet access and a twenty-three inch flat screen TV mounted into the bulkhead.

For reasons I cannot fully understand, Lonnie Turner became my best friend. Lonnie is retired from the military as well as the Washington DC Police Department. Basically, most of my life entails working, sailing and getting involved in adventures at the marina.

There are, of course, other aspects of my existence, including being a die-hard New York Yankees fan trying in vain to root for the Tampa Bay Rays. It's not easy being me.

Cuban Exile

As far as getting involved with dockside adventures, it's a mystery to me. My goal in coming to Florida was to lead a nice quiet life taking care of my customers and helping out my friends. For reasons that escape me entirely, things just seem to happen around me. These things grab a hold of me and all of a sudden I'm up to my waist in some sordid affair that leads me into places I really shouldn't be.

Hey, it's a lot better than going to sales status meetings at some large technology company. Given all of that, my life is pretty good. My love life is not necessarily a stable one. I had managed to drive off two good women due, in part, from my reluctance to truly settle down. I just seem to get caught up in things that are not conducive to a healthy relationship. My current effort at achieving boyfriend status involves Carla, the dock master at Key West Marina. We met awhile back when I took an extended trip through the Florida Keys and the Bahamas.

Carla was in her early forties and had been dock master for enough years to give me advice on how to back into a slip in a heavy wind. She had jet black hair that framed a cupie doll face and complemented her curvy shape. She always seemed to wear khaki shorts and a halter top except in the winter when she wore khaki shorts and a halter top with a jacket.

I snapped back from self analysis and poured two mugs of coffee. Basically, we were ready to sail. We really didn't need Sam and DeeDee for crew. We were well provisioned and the boat was in perfect shape. So, I said to Lonnie, "How about it? Should we just stay with our plan and head for Key West?" I heard a grunt with a positive tone to it so I took that for a yes.

By 10 AM we were 'lines away' leaving *Venice Yacht Club* for Key West.

Chapter 5

When we were close to the entrance to Key West, I called Carla to let her know I was coming in. She told me we would have a slip at the end of the dock; a nice quiet spot about fifty yards or so away from the bars and restaurants. That suited us nicely.

A little while later we eased into a slip as Carla looked on. She brought her ever-present clipboard as well as her beautiful smile.

Lonnie threw her a bow line that she quickly tied onto the cleat on the dock. Then he stepped to the stern and threw her a stern line. We were all tied up, nice and neat, within ten minutes.

Carla jumped on board and gave me a big welcome back hug. Lonnie went below and neatened up the cabin. I finally let go of Carla and eased over to the cockpit area. I opened the cooler and pulled out three Heinekens and we celebrated our arrival. Sam and DeeDee were missing the best part of the trip.

Some people from the marina came over and joined us. It really doesn't take much to get a good party together in Key West. Someone brought over a bottle of rum – ice could be heard with its distinctive 'klink klink' sound.

The noise level rose. Someone turned up the stereo. People who we had never met were trying to become our best friends. The evening wore on with much laughter and merriment. I left Lonnie in charge of the boat and disappeared down the pier with Carla at my side. It was good to be back in the Keys.

***

Carla Ramos and I met in Key West a year or so ago. She is a native-born Cuban who managed to make it out of Fidel's paradise and into the states. She was brought over to the US in 1973 as a five-year-old child and had been raised by her mother's sister.

Carla's parents were jailed and possibly executed in 1972 on a charge of spying for the US. Her older brother by fifteen years, Ernesto, managed to get them to the US mainland via an illegal flotilla. For a child, she remembered quite a bit about the flotilla especially the shooting and screaming on board the escape vessel as they got into a gun battle with the Cuban Navy in the Florida Straits.

People in the flotilla huddled down trying to save themselves from being shot or drowned. After what seemed like an eternity, the Cuban Navy gave up its chase and the escape boat miraculously reached the shores of Miami Beach.

She recalled people fighting the current as they made their way to the beach. They were scattering in all directions, desperately trying to reach what they believed would be a better life.

As they approached Miami, Carla remembered her brother bravely carrying her through chest-deep water and onto the shore. Somehow, amidst all of that chaos, she felt her toes hit the sand and knew that she was about to start a new life.

Cuban Exile

In Carla's eyes, her brother would forever be a hero. For reasons that her young mind did not understand, she and her brother separated on that beachfront in the dark of night. Carla was brought to her aunt – wondering if she would ever see her brother again.

She often speculated about his being arrested by the Cuban Government or possibly going off the grid in fear of being captured for illegal trafficking. Carla thought that he might have been part of a ring that relocated people to the States.

Her only communication with Ernesto came indirectly through their aunt. His loss was with her every day of her life. We talked about her brother many times and the possible paths that his secretive life may have taken.

This speculation ended recently, as Carla's aunt lay on her death bed in Miami. After all these years, her aunt finally revealed to her what had happened to Carla's brother.

Chapter 6

Ernesto Ramos was a brave man. He was determined to give his sister a better life – a life of freedom – a life filled with hopes and dreams rather than the pre-determined mundane existence that the Communists offered. He risked his life for his little sister as a Cuban patrol boat fired on its own countrymen.

On the night that Ernesto smuggled his little sister into the US, a gunfight ensued between the refugee escape boat and a Cuban patrol boat. He tried to shield Carla from the bullets that were flying in all directions. He covered her tiny body with his own.

During the gun battle, Ernesto shot and wounded a Cuban Naval Officer. The Cuban patrol boat left the skirmish and headed back to Havana in an effort to save the wounded officer. It was too little too late and the officer died. As a result, Ernesto was wanted for murder in Cuba. Ramos knew that if he was captured in Cuba, it would mean certain execution.

Shorty after he reached the US and safety for his little sister, Ernesto disappeared into the criminal underground that was Miami in the nineteen seventies.

He was involved in a few drug deals until one went bad – shots were fired – someone lay dead. Ernesto became a wanted man in both Miami and Cuba.

His aunt helped him with forged documents and a Florida driver's license under the name of *Ernesto Clemente*. Ernesto's favorite baseball player in the States was Roberto Clemente. In fact, he himself had played minor league baseball for awhile. Carla kept her family name -- Ramos.

Every once in awhile Ernesto spoke to his aunt – never revealing his location – never revealing his profession – always sounding like he was on the move.

Still, he never let a phone call end without asking about Carla – right up to the very end of his aunt's life. Finally, Ernesto contacted his sister himself and explained why he was underground for all of these years.

Back in 1973, when the flotilla landed, Ernesto went off the grid leaving his sister to his aunt. He had only a few dollars and a will to survive. The death of a Miami drug dealer forced him underground. He wound up doing menial jobs and leading a reclusive life style.

Clemente moved around a lot – staying clear of the law – bouncing around between Florida, the Bahamas and the Virgin Islands. His secretive life led him to become an expert at forged documentation. But modern computer systems were bearing down on him in Miami.

He had several close calls over his identity and was almost captured twice in the last year. At age fifty-eight, he was tired of changing identities and tired of running. He re-entered Cuba for the first time in thirty years and settled into a quiet life of crewing on tourist boats in Mariel.

He shared with his sister the single driving force that lived within him – the reason he had returned to his homeland. He wanted to find out what had happened to their mother and father.

Then he would return to Florida and get himself cleared of the now ancient drug killing. He asked Carla to help him with his repatriation effort.

Chapter 7

Carla had overcome the trauma of her early childhood and was a delight to be around. She lived in a small apartment above the marina office. She could stand in her kitchen and look out over the boats in their slips. Sometimes, when we came out of the shower, we would stand in the kitchen, wrapped up in towels and gaze down at the boats. I would mix some drinks and she would recite the make and model of each boat as well as its expected stay.

Carla could also tell you quirky things about the owners. Hey, no one in Key West is totally normal! She also had a side job that consisted of taking out boats for absentee owners who wanted their vessels exercised for one reason or another – testing new equipment – checking out engine repairs – or just plain running the engines. There is always something needing tender, loving care on a boat.

Once, in the small hours, where night meets morning, we watched a couple who performed in the Duval Street female impersonation show, try to board a sixty-five foot yacht.

The owner was trying to help them but they had on skirts that were so tight they just couldn't negotiate the boarding ladder – so they took the skirts off! There they stood; men who looked a lot like women with only underwear on –standing on the pier. Of course, it was women's underwear.

One had Marilyn Monroe attire on complete with a tight sequin-laden top – tits the size of grapefruits. The other one had on a Cher getup complete with really long black hair. Where else could you find this type of entertainment right out your window?

Carla and I loved our time together, but that was as far as it went for both of us. We each had a lot of mileage on ourselves. Sometimes I thought about my ex-wife, Nancy, living up in Manhattan. We were about as far apart as any two people could be. I really don't like to think of her at all; so I don't. I do think of my childhood sweetheart, Jane, as well as my recent vector into singledom, Carmen.

All of this can get complicated and I don't like complications. I am an expert in avoidance techniques, so I put them all aside. As for now, I was sipping dark rum on ice with a lime wedge. We stared at the boats for awhile longer before Carla let her towel drop to the floor.

***

A few days easily slipped by. Lonnie and I settled into a routine of going to the gym followed by a healthy walk through town. All roads lead to Duval Street, so after about three days or so, one has seen it all.

Strange as it may seem, despite being in the party capitol of the world, I managed to get some work done for my marina software business. I checked in on a half dozen marinas and drummed up some new business that I quickly dropped in the lap of my partner, Ed Dowd.

Cuban Exile

I am more of a global thinker whereas Ed is a 'down-to-Earth' pragmatist. He is most helpful when software problems arise. I am most helpful at taking clients out to lunch. It makes for a pretty good partnership. He handles the company finances but, to my knowledge doesn't really adhere to *Generally Accepted Accounting Practices*. Sometimes he tells me that we have a 'cash flow' problem. The last time he said that, I asked him, "So where does the cash flow to?"

"Oh, it flows in and out of different accounts."

"Uh … by any chance, does some of it flow to the IRS?"

"I suppose, in a sense, it does."

I mean, what do you say to a guy who gives answers like that? I try not to ask too many questions about our company finances. I had this secret fear that Ed would one day disappear leaving me with this so-called *cash flow problem*. I could easily picture him sipping drinks with tiny umbrellas in them on the coast of a small Caribbean country that is not necessarily part of the United Nations. Like my ex-wife, I try not to think about it.

Chapter 8

After hanging in Key West for a little over a week, Lonnie and I were getting antsy to do something. One day, upon arriving back to the boat from a meeting with one of my clients, I found Lonnie below decks. He was sitting at the navigation station. Nautical charts were spread all over the navigation table and had spilled over to the main table in the saloon. I sat down on the ladder steps and peered in below. "We headed for somewhere?"

"You won't believe this. I just got the surprise phone call of my life."

"Yeah? Do tell."

"Sam Feldman just called me and he wants us to take the boat to Cuba!"

"What?"

"Yeah, Cuba. The Cuban medical powers that be want Sam to teach them how to work with burn victims – some kind of medical symposium."

"You're serious, right?"

"Serious is not the right word. I am ecstatic! We get to sail where we've never gone before and help some people out at the same time. The whole thing is being supported and funded by *Doctors Without Borders.* Sam apparently has a lot more juice that we have given him credit for."

Lonnie went on about Sam making arrangements at Mariel Harbor Marina. Sam went ahead and had us cleared for entry due to assisting the local medical authorities along with Doctors Without Borders. We also had hotel accommodations if we wanted them. What could be wrong with this mission?

Nothing! We could leave in a day or two depending on the weather.

Sam would already be in Cuba by the time we arrived. He had some medical supplies shipped to us here in Key West that we would take to Cuba rather than risk them being stolen.

He wanted to sail back to Key West with us when he was finished with his mission. He also said he might bring DeeDee along for the sail. Hmmmm.

"I think I see where this is going."

"You should, Genius." Lonnie looked all around the cabin as if he had lost something. Finally, he said, "Hey, take a look at these charts. We have been up and down the west coast of Florida numerous times. We have been through plenty of stops in the Keys and we've run over to the Bahamas a few times. We even went out to the Tortugas. Cuba is the last stop for us. It completes us as sailors."

"I'll drink to that."

Chapter 9

On the morning that we chose to leave Key West, there was a cold chill-filled breeze blowing from the North. It was March and most of the east coast was still enveloped in winter.

I took in the conditions for a minute and then went below decks to look for a warm jacket to wear. My sailing jacket collection is famous throughout the west coast of Florida. Today I chose a navy blue and yellow *Gill* selection. It was sturdy enough to serve as foul weather gear but not so heavy that you would be sweating into it when afternoon came calling. It also had five or six zippered pockets to put things in … a hand held GPS, a strobe light, in case you went overboard and, of course, the ubiquitous iPhone.

Through the portals, I could see Carla coming down the dock. She was half running and half walking towards the boat slip. She had her arms wrapped around herself as if that would keep her warm.

When she reached the boat, she pulled on the bow line, hopped over the railing, grabbed onto a mast stay and made her way to the cockpit. This she did in one smooth continuous motion. Carla could glide around a boat with the ease and self assuredness of an Olympic ice skater.

She reached the companionway, turned around and used the ladder rails to slide below into the cabin – kind of like a fireman when the alarm sounds. We stood there looking at each other as the morning sun made its way through the marina and initiated the daily squawking of the sea gulls. We held on to each other, but only for a moment. I hate long goodbyes and it seems that Carla did too.

She reached into her back pocket and pulled out my final marina bill. "Sign here, Sailor," she said. "We'll bill your home office later this month."

She hugged me again and then reversed her path up the companionway, over the railing and back up onto the dock. I watched her walk down the dock to the marina office. It was not an unpleasant sight.

Lonnie and I finished loading provisions onto the boat and made one last check of the weather before we shoved off. We were 'lines away' at 8AM as we made way towards the Key West Sea Buoy and then out into the Florida Straits – destination - Mariel Harbor, Cuba.

Chapter 10

Leaving for an extended sailing trip always gives me the anxiety associated with things unknown along with the challenge attached to dealing with the elements. The elements are always there -- demanding your immediate attention -- changing at will – painting a new picture to dwell on before you finished the old one.

Sailing is an extension of your reach in life. It is at once exhilarating, fulfilling and tranquil. If you let it, sailing can reach deeply inside of you. It can take you to a place that opens up into the sheer joy of having cooperated with the forces of nature to achieve your objective of going from point A to point B – a beautiful thing. Someone once described it to me as long periods of peace and serenity punctuated by moments of sheer, stark terror.

Lonnie and I were anticipating a trip of approximately twenty hours or so depending on winds, tides, currents and who knows what? The trip itself was about a hundred nautical miles.

Mariel lay approximately due southwest of our current position that was leading us out of Key West. The weather was postcard perfect and the water at once light blue and turquoise green.

After about four hours into the sail, we were dozing, reading and talking. I brought up some sandwiches from the galley and we ate and navigated at the same time! We checked and re-checked our safety gear and electronics before settling into a simple two hour watch -- two hours on and two hours off. We kept to the watch schedule -- more or less.

We sailed on through the Gulf of Mexico into what could only be described as a soft, easy beam reach. The wind blew along the center of the boat and pushed us forward in an effortless manner. We headed south.

Lonnie was not only a great sailor but also was an excellent conversationalist. His favorite topics were about military history. It seemed only natural, what with heading to Cuba and all, that we fell into a discussion about the *Cuban Missile Crisis*.

I was definitely aware of its place in the history books, having taken a few American History courses in high school and in college. I just didn't have the detailed knowledge that Lonnie had. As with all things military, he seemed to possess a myriad of facts and figures about the Crisis.

This, of course, made for the perfect sailing companion as we set our course towards to Cuba. Lonnie talked about the Crisis. "Yeah, I remember it pretty well. I was sixteen years old – going to high school in Florida. You'd think the world was headed for another war. There were thousands of troops moving into South Florida – tanks, missiles, jeeps, planes. You name it.

"Well, in many ways we *were* headed for a full scale war – this time with nuclear weapons. President Kennedy stared down the Russians and avoided a global fiasco. Millions of lives would have been lost had Kennedy not acted with both diplomacy and military strategy to save the planet."

I turned to Lonnie and said, "What happened - did JFK ignore Marilyn for a few days?" Well, the way he came back at me, I might as well had run for cover if there was any place to run. I realized I had pushed the wrong button.

"Listen Genius, Kennedy had the courage, the nerve and the drive to save us from global annihilation. All these stories about women are nothing more than half truths and innuendo perpetrated by the press.

"Kennedy saved our asses. The man was a decorated war hero for God's sake. Didn't you ever hear of the '*PT 109*'? Just like he did during World War II, he stepped up to the plate and dug his heels in. He stood tall during the greatest crisis our country has ever known.

"All you have to contribute are some possibly true stories about Marilyn Monroe? Well you, my friend, ought to be made of better stuff than that!

"Without JFK I might not be here telling you all of this. Kennedy was my childhood hero. Were there a few women around? Probably. Lots of Presidents had extracurricular activities going on. Kennedy never let that get in the way of being President. So I don't want to hear another word about Marilyn or any other women. He saved us. Why don't you contemplate that instead of the rest of the bull you've been touting?"

Well, I certainly handled that one deftly. Lonnie grunted in my direction and then went below to take a nap. I went back to the steering wheel and checked our course and position. Everything looked good. I made a mental note not to criticize JFK again and continued through the Florida Straits on towards Cuba.

Cuban Exile

As I recalled from college, there were a lot of players involved in the Cuban Missile Crisis, including a full contingent of our highest ranking military officers. Secretary of Defense Robert McNamara was, of course, deeply involved as was the President's brother, Attorney General Robert Kennedy.

The Joint Chiefs of Staff and their fellow military compadres, wanted to see blood on the tracks. They begged the President to invade and hold the island nation of Cuba. They also were willing to fire upon any Russian ships that approached Cuban waters. History maintains that Soviet Premier Nikita Khrushchev was being heavily pressured by his own military to take more aggressive action towards the US including the use of nuclear missiles.

About a year or so before the Crisis, there were Soviet diesel-powered submarines, armed with nuclear warheads, cruising around the Florida Straits. It's hard to say how many and what their mission was but they were out there -- very close by – hauling around nuclear weapons.

The Florida Straits is a body of water that is kind of like a big pass through. It connects the Gulf of Mexico with the Atlantic Ocean. Leaving Key West and heading towards Cuba requires a vessel to cross the Florida Straits.

The Straits form a backwards L-shaped configuration that separates Florida from the Bahamas and Cuba. Its southern waters open westward into the Gulf of Mexico, while its northern part opens into the Atlantic Ocean. Because the Straits form an intersection of these large waterways, it provides an important and productive environment for marine biodiversity.

Sandy Mason

Way back when, Benjamin Franklin got interested in the Straits. At that time he was our Postmaster General. So, in between harnessing electricity and inventing bifocals, he authorized his cousin, a whaling captain, to draw up a map of the Gulf Stream to improve mail delivery between the colonies and England. The map shows the current beginning between southern Florida and the Bahamas.

The Straits is where Nazi submarines hung out during World War II and where the Soviet subs played cat and mouse with American vessels during the cold war.

After the 1959 revolution in Cuba, good old Fidel decided to cast his lot with the Ruskies. He sold a lot of sugar and cigars while the Soviets built themselves a nice little series of missile sites. The problem with the sites was that the Soviets ultimately put long-range nuclear missiles on them. They covered them all up with tree branches. Brilliant! It didn't take the US government too long to figure this out and that's when the Crisis took shape. I thought about the Florida Straits and the events leading up to the Crisis ...

Cuban Exile

April 1961 - The United States of America

President Kennedy Ordered the ill-fated Bay of Pigs Invasion.

Roger Maris and Mickey Mantle Began their historic Home Run chase of Babe Ruth's record of sixty – set in 1927.

Ernest Hemingway continued to write even though he suffered badly from the depression that eventually brought him to suicide.

Elvis was shooting 'Blue Hawaii'

Frank Sinatra released 'Swing Along With Me'.

Cuban leader Fidel Castro openly declares that he is a Marxist-Leninist. He allies himself with Nikita Khrushchev and Soviet Russia.

Russian engineers raced to complete the K-19 nuclear submarine.

Chapter 11

The weather was cooperating beautifully as we approached the final few hours of daylight. I heard a rumbling sound in the galley as Lonnie put on a pot of coffee. A few minutes later he came up topside and handed me a steaming mug. "Thanks.", I said. He just grunted. I guess he was still aggravated with me over the JFK – Marilyn thing. This time I was smart enough to keep my mouth shut.

When I was a school kid about ten years old or so, we had a special project in history class. Each of us had to select a US President and recite from memory a portion of that President's inaugural address. I chose Jack Kennedy. Even at that age, I could sense him defining our commitment to democracy …

'Let the word go forth from this time and place to friend and foe alike that the torch has been passed to a new generation of Americans

– born in this century, tempered by war, disciplined by a hard and bitter peace, proud of our ancient heritage—and unwilling to witness or permit the slow undoing of those human rights to which this nation has always been committed.' …

Cuban Exile

As a ten year old, I thought *"Wow! Jack Kennedy must have been the coolest President ever.* I mean, when I was ten, Lyndon Johnson was President. He looked like a carnival barker in a bad suit. At that time any President would have been an improvement. But Kennedy, aside from his good looks and charm, had an even stronger message to convey …

> *'Let every nation know, whether it wishes us well or ill, that we shall pay any price, bear any burden, meet any hardship, support any friend, oppose any foe, in order to assure the survival and the success of liberty.'...*

I thought, as a boy, there was Jack Kennedy telling any nation in the world that we would kick their collective asses if they tried to take us on in the fight for liberty and freedom. Well, I delivered JFK's inaugural address and got an 'A' on my project. I wondered if I should tell Lonnie about the grade school history project. Nah.

Chapter 12

The wind had picked up so we decided to reef our sails. It was getting closer to sundown so it was a good move. That way, if something came up at night, we wouldn't have to go up on deck and shorten sail. I steered into the wind while Lonnie pulled down a portion of the mainsail and tied it up. He was now talking to me again. Nobody can really stay mad at me for any length of time. I'm just too likeable!

We were both mindful of the two-hour watch. Lonnie was 'on' and I was 'off' for the next couple of hours. I went below, reached up to the electrical panel and switched on the running lights. I lay down in my bunk and fell asleep thinking about the Cuban Missile Crisis. It was about 7 PM. We had about another ten hours or so before reaching the Mariel Sea Buoy.

The Cuban Missile Crisis was an extraordinary time in the Cold War, the war that I grew up with. It was the closest the world had ever come to total nuclear disaster. As far back as December 1961, US Intelligence began to monitor Soviet vessel traffic into and out of Cuba. We watched the build-up over a period of a few months.

On September 13, 1962, Kennedy, at a news conference, put the full blame for placing nuclear weapons, ninety miles from our shores, squarely in the Soviet camp. He railed at the Castro government, criticizing it as an economic failure, propped up by a ruthless dictator who openly betrayed his own people.

Jack pulled no punches as he made clear his position as Commander in Chief of all US military forces …

'… this country will do whatever must be done to protect its own security and that of its allies.'

In October 1962, JFK ordered U-2 spy-plane photography to take place over the island of Cuba. One of our pilots was shot down and killed during the infamous "thirteen days" of October – the days when the Crisis was at its boiling point. The pilot, Rudolph Anderson, flew several surveillance missions over Cuba before being shot down. President Kennedy posthumously awarded him the Air Force Cross.

Anderson made photographs that provided the US government with conclusive evidence of the introduction of long-range offensive missiles into Cuba. The missiles were not simply defensive weapons such as 'Surface To Air' missiles but strategic long range missiles carrying nuclear warheads capable of blowing every one of us into smithereens!

President Kennedy was not going to sit still for this. He confronted the Russians, along with Soviet Premier Nikita Khrushchev, about the missiles. After all, this was John F. Kennedy they were screwing with – a war hero – the de facto leader of the 'Free World'. Even though the nuclear warheads, that the Soviets installed, provided the capability to kill untold millions via the power of mutually assured destruction, Kennedy would not back down. Although his military faction wanted an invasion of Cuba, Kennedy thought otherwise.

He decided on a much wiser course of action than invading Cuba. He tempered his military people yet remained adamant that the Soviets remove the missiles. To accomplish his goal, the President ordered a naval 'quarantine' of Cuba and moved to stop the flow of new weapons into Cuba.

The President also went on national television on the evening of October 26, 1962 to inform the public of the developments in Cuba.

This included his decision to initiate and enforce the 'quarantine'. Staring into the young President's soul were the potential global consequences if the Crisis continued to escalate. The tone of the President's remarks was dead serious and the message unmistakable. The decision that he made had placed the entire planet in his hands. The President went ahead and cited a modern day version of the Monroe Doctrine ...

> ... *'It shall be the policy of this nation to regard any nuclear missile launched from Cuba against any nation in the Western Hemisphere as an attack by the Soviet Union on the United States ...'*

The President then pulled out all the stops and ordered the military to a state of readiness of DEFCON 2. US Naval Forces began implementation of the quarantine and plans accelerated for a military strike on Cuba.

A lesser man would have folded under such pressure to initiate a global war. Instead of folding, the

President took full control of the situation and coaxed the Russians away from nuclear war by offering to remove our missiles from Turkey.

The generals, advisors, consultants and secretaries wanted the United States to declare war on the Soviet Union. Kennedy pushed them all aside. He knew in his heart that Americans did not want nuclear war. They wanted to save their way of life.

Chapter 13

This trip was turning out to be a soft and easy ride into Mariel Harbor.

It was still Lonnie's turn for watch duty but I came up into the cockpit anyway. Everything is different on the water at night. Familiar shapes such as cargo ships, commercial fishing vessels and cruise ships take on new meaning as you navigate through the night. An extra pair of eyes is always welcome.

I poured some coffee as we both took in a gray-black sea topped off by a starry sky. We were quiet for awhile as I wondered what it must have been like to be aboard ship on these very waters in October 1962 – the height of the Cuban Missile Crisis.

I asked Lonnie, "So what do all these DEFCON levels really mean?"

"Well, they indicate a military state of readiness associated with a threat to the country. Currently we list five different states of readiness. It's just a simple way to describe what's going on out there with regard to national security. Funny thing is, the DEFCON levels go in reverse order as the threat level increases."

"What?" Some freighters passed us off the starboard side bow. I gave them plenty of room.

"DEFCON means defense readiness condition or something close to that. You know, it means 'heads up' out there."

"Yeah but what do all the levels actually mean?"

"Okay, as much as I can remember, DEFCON 5 is a good thing. It basically means we are in peacetime so all is well, happy days are here again and so on and so forth. Just keep your eyes open."

"Great, I like DEFCON 5. Something tells me that DEFCON 4 is not as much fun."

"Right, Genius. DEFCON 4 means something might be up, so we should increase intelligence gathering and security measures. With the War on Terror we seem to go on and off from DEFCON 4 to DEFCON 5."

"Hmm, I never noticed."

"I'm not surprised. Now DEFCON 3 is serious. It is designated for situations such as post 911. It actually calls for an immediate Armed Forces readiness and I think the Air Force is supposed to mobilize in fifteen or twenty minutes -- something like that."

"How the hell does an outfit as big as the Air Force get ready in fifteen minutes? I can't even get up and dressed in fifteen minutes."

"I don't know. Maybe they sleep in their cockpits with their helmets in their laps? My point is, Genius, the Air Force is hustling big time to save your ass."

"I am honored. Okay, how about DEFCON 2 and DEFCON 1?"

"They are for near wartime - maximum readiness – all hands on deck – battle stations – say your prayers. You know, dead serious events are upon us."

"Did we go to DEFCON 2 during the Cuban Missile Crisis?"

"The short answer is 'Yup, we did.'. In fact different branches of the military can be issued different DEFCON levels. For instance, during the Cuban

Missile Crisis, that is generally considered one of the most dangerous moments in American military history, the Strategic Air Command went on DEFCON 2, while the rest of the military went on DEFCON 3. It can get complicated."

Chapter 14

We made it to within a mile or so off Mariel Harbor in the middle of the night. In the blackness we could see the lights of the town. The inlet was too treacherous to attempt in the dark. I took the wheel and made some long and wide 'lazy eights' to kill the time before we made ready to tie up in Mariel.

As I circled, I wondered what kind of reception we would receive from the locals. I hoped that Sam had already paved our way through the administrative red tape with our good neighbors to the south. Not that I expected to be greeted as a hero – although that would be fine with me – you know, a small parade – maybe some dancing girls and a couple of floats.

Lonnie took hold of our marine radio. He tuned in to channel sixteen as it crackled with static.

"Sailing vessel *Epithelia* hailing Mariel Marina." After a few seconds, he repeated … "Sailing vessel *Epithelia* hailing Mariel Marina." A marine operator responded in English. "I read you, *Epithelia*, please switch to channel seven one."

"Roger that Mariel – switching to seven one." We had contacted the marina and now had moved to another radio frequency in order to free up the busy traffic on channel sixteen. After what seemed to me to be a long time, we heard …

"*Epithelia*, how many souls on board?"

"Mariel, we have two souls on board. We are on a medical mercy mission sponsored by Doctors Without Borders. We have official clearance from the Cuban Security Police allowing us to enter and dock. Please direct us to a slip accommodating a thirty-eight foot vessel."

The Cubans seemed to want to take charge. "*Epithelia*, stand by, we will direct you as ordered by our shore side naval commander. Maintain your position until directed otherwise. List the names of all who are on board."

Well, they seemed to get all huffy about approaching the marina … Wow, the *shore side naval commander.* Sam must have pulled some weight to get us an official shore side naval commander.

We waited …

***

The Cubans made us wait through a nap and two Heinekens before they crackled the radio again. "*Epithelia*, this is Mariel Marina, you are cleared for entry through to our inspection process. Please proceed toward red buoy two and follow the Police boat to your slip. You will remain on board through inspection. Mariel out."

Okay then, it was welcome to Cuba for us – time to celebrate and party down, just like they do in Key West … not exactly. The 'inspectors' as they called themselves were a total pain in the ass. In addition, they moved about their tasks with all the speed of a row boat loaded down with Cuban exiles.

Two armed guards boarded our boat and gave us the once over. We were well prepared with passports and other required papers. The guards took our papers and passed them up to a guy in a white uniform with lots of medals and awards dripping off of him. With that, the guards went below and started nosing around. One of them grabbed a plastic container labeled …

'Medical Supplies - Sterilized'

'For A Sanitized Area Only.'

I yelled up to the pier in the direction of Mr. Whitesuit, "Why don't you leave that stuff as is until you clear us? These cartons are the property of Doctors Without Borders. We have clearance to deliver them to Cuban officials from Doctors Without Borders." Mr. Whitesuit just snarled at me. He signaled to one of his men to hand up one of the cartons. I addressed him again, "Hey, don't you get it General? Medical supplies – ¿Necesitas reservas medicas. We were at an impasse. Both of us doing a mano a mano stare down.

Cuban Exile

It was during this macho man confrontation that I saw Sam running down the dock wearing his official doctor whites. He was followed by two uniformed Cuban Security Police. Little old five-foot-seven Sam was yelling at Mr. Whitesuit. "Hey, asshole! Can't you read? Medical supplies – get it – medical supplies. Leave them the fuck alone!"

Wow, this was like the cavalry coming in on an old western movie, complete with a hero who stood his ground against some bad guys. I didn't think Sam had that in him. He went toe to toe with Mr. Whitesuit as he waved some official looking papers in his face. "Check it out, Admiral, and get your men off of my vessel. Here's all the clearance documentation you'll ever need … and as I just said, get your men off of my vessel … NOW!"

Whitesuit backed down and Sam boarded his boat and gave huge bear hugs to Lonnie and me while the Cuban inspectors disembarked. Sam's escorts then boarded, located our goods and brought them to an awaiting van.

Sam brought with him two satellite phones and two satellite internet cards that fit nicely into a slot on our laptops. Sam even had a hidden spot on *Epithelia* for the satellite phones just in case someone went snooping around.

Internet access in Cuba was not the best. Having a direct satellite connection made life easier.

I just saw a whole new side of Sam. He took charge of our docking arrangements, brought in the medical supplies and hid away our satellite links in a secure location. It was definitely time for a drink. Sam was about to go off duty. We toasted a successful

landing and a huge one-upsmanship victory over
Whitesuit and his boys.

Chapter 15

After all that time aboard *Epithelia*, Lonnie and I were glad to settle into a hotel. Sam deserted us for a nearby Hilton while we stayed at the much smaller, but much friendlier Mariel Marina Inn. We booked two adjoining rooms so we could cross-talk if we wanted. The *Epithelia*, although a comfortable boat, couldn't compete with a full size bathroom and a big screen TV. I stretched out on the king size bed and promptly fell asleep.

Lonnie woke me up a few hours later and I got cleaned up for dinner. I wasn't sure what they wear for dinner in Cuba but I figured jeans and a white dress shirt would be fine. I was right. We walked around the Mariel Marina district and found a restaurant to our liking. It had pictures over the bar of Ernest Hemingway.

One of them showed Hemingway in a drink toasting stance – raising his arm so it stretched out towards the ocean. He had a huge grin and appeared to be totally at one with this place – a far cry from the guy who committed suicide only a few years later.

Someone once asked Hemingway how he developed into being a writer. To that he replied, "Because all you have to do when you write fiction is sit in front of a typewriter and bleed." The guy was definitely intense. I'm not sure if I would ever have it in me to write a book, but you never know.

Ernest Hemingway had made his home in Cuba from 1939 to 1960. He loved the sound of the waves crashing over the seawall that defined Havana. It was here that he had written seven books, including *The Old Man and the Sea, A Moveable Feast and Islands in the Stream*. He wrote with guts, flare and passion -- fueled by rum and guided by the pulse of the vibrant city that he loved.

After dinner we continued our tour. The Cuban people were friendly and gracious hosts; of course, greenback dollars didn't hurt.

There were far too many prostitutes walking the streets and they were far too young. It was sad actually, seeing girls just out of grade school trying to balance themselves in high heels. We had almost enough celebrating for one day and decided to head back to our hotel.

We passed through the lobby and out to a veranda overlooking the marina. It was a hot and steamy night with dead air penetrating the veranda. We sat at the bar that was nicely cooled by overhead fans.

We could hear people from the deck nearby talking and laughing -- genuinely enjoying the evening. The bartender, who appeared to be about eighty years old, was entertaining his audience. When he returned to the bar, we traded small talk before he slipped away to cater to some new customers. He welcomed them like they were long lost family. A guy in a beige crumpled linen suit stumbled over to the bar, sat close to us. He ordered Stolis on the rocks.

Without any introduction, he began talking to us. He had a weird accent that sounded like English, Spanish and Central European all wrapped up in one. We traded names and some small talk before he told us he was from both Cuba and Russia. His name was

Andrei Pavnara and he had grown up mostly here in Cuba and partially back home in Russia. He looked tired, sullen and pretty drunk. He was babbling about his childhood and his father and some other stuff that made no sense to me. Oh well, I thought, "*Welcome to Cuba.*"

Our new friend was generously buying drinks that we hadn't even touched. He gazed off into somewhere and pointed out to something or other towards the town. Believe me, when a hard drinking, fast talking guy switches from Russian to Spanish at will, you know you're in for a tough conversation.

Mostly, I liked the way he stared off in silence. I was secretly hoping for more of this. Apparently, from what I could decipher, he had a pretty important job, something about dealing with nuclear material of some sort. I really couldn't follow him very well and neither could Lonnie. This guy was definitely ruining our first night in Cuba! The bad news was that he was staying in the same hotel as we were – only a few doors down.

Chapter 16

Andrei Pavnara ordered vodka as he stared at himself in the mirror behind the bar. This he did in a manner where he appeared to be looking at both Lonnie and me as he spoke. He spoke into the mirror, this time in perfect English.

"Have you ever heard of the accident that occurred on the Soviet nuclear submarine K-19? It happened in 1961." I did not, but Lonnie answered, "Yeah, I think so. I was a kid when it actually took place, but I remember the news stories that they put out years later."

"Of course it was years later. It was all hush hush at the time."

"What exactly happened?" I asked. Andrei proceeded to tell us about this Soviet nuclear submarine. This time he used English so I felt obligated to listen. Still, I wondered why a guy would go off on Soviet era nuclear submarines to two perfect strangers.

Anyway, he began, "The K-19 was a huge technological advance for the Soviet Navy. It was built specifically to provide the Soviet Union with nuclear weapons capability at sea. The government ordered it built at a pace that ignored testing and safety for the workers as well as (later on) for the crew. At least eight workers died as a result of accidents while building the nuclear powered submarine.

"The pace of construction caused mistakes to be made, especially with respect to the nuclear reactors. The Soviet Navy was under extreme pressure to complete the vessel. There was no backup cooling system. The K-19's mechanics were told the reactor was already too complex.

"In spite of this, naval crewmen were thrilled to be part of the maiden voyage. These men were the elite of the Soviet Navy and were ready to take the helm."

The present-day Russian standing next to us ordered another round of vodka for everyone. I must admit, I pushed mine away. No one is better at downing vodka than the Ruskies. I could not compete nor did I want to. We got silent for awhile, thinking about the K-19.

A pretty blonde woman entered the bar and passed us by without a glance. She took a table way in the back of the room and opened up a menu. She was blonde, slender and attractive.

Her presence temporarily halted my curiosity about the K-19. I still didn't understand why Pavnara was telling us all of this. I was just about to escape to my hotel room when Lonnie put his hand up in a stop sign gesture signaling that I should hang out and listen to the end of the story.

The ancient bartender looked at me and smiled. He walked over to us, feigning wiping off the bar. He then made a circular motion with his forefinger indicating that the Russian was not quite right in the head.

Andrei Pavnara ignored him and continued with his K-19 monologue. "The K-19 used to hide from its own fellow submarines as part of training exercises. On June 4, 1961, the K-19 was hiding in the North Atlantic from Soviet diesel subs. A cracked pipe burst and the reactor room temperature exceeded one hundred forty degrees. The radiation level was also rising. The reactor had to be cooled.

"The captain asked for volunteers to save the sub. Twenty-two men volunteered. Several lost their lives. The remaining men saved the reactor from exploding by fixing the cooling system.

Those men suffered horrible radiation sickness. They died begging their shipmates to kill them. Their skin literally peeled away from their bodies. It wasn't until 1991 that we admitted to the accident at sea."

I was stunned listening to this story. I asked Andrei why he was here in Cuba. "I am a doctor specializing in helping burn victims as well as those suffering from radiation sickness.

I was at Chernobyl in 1986. I know first-hand what radiation can do. My father was a young naval officer on the K-19. He told me about the crew and the radiation sickness that followed. He pleaded with the Soviet Naval brass to put in additional safety measures on the nuclear subs.

The Soviet authorities pushed aside my father's concerns and continued to build nuclear powered submarines that placed their crews in danger. Because of his strong stance on safety issues, he was shunned by his own submarine corp. He was ridiculed as a coward who wouldn't stand up to the American capitalists.

Because of my father's experiences with radiation sickness, I knew, early on, that I would become a doctor.

"I saw you both at the marina entry checkpoint earlier today. I was about to render assistance when Dr. Feldman came by. He seemed to handle himself well so I left for the restaurant. You see? I am a Cuban citizen attending the medical conference. I'm primarily here to assist Cuban medical students in treating victims afflicted with serious burns or if needed, radiation sickness. I will be delivering lectures and providing case studies at the conference. I'm part of a medical team from Doctors Without Borders. I am also a friend of Sam Feldman."

Chapter 17

The next morning both Lonnie and I slept long and late. I showered and got ready for the day by ordering a huge room service breakfast. I also ordered enough coffee to crash through even the most pronounced of vodka hangovers. We both had brought our laptops to the hotel. I fired mine up and waited for the room service attendant to arrive.

We did not have a busy schedule at all – only touring around, doing a little cosmetic boat work on *Epithelia* and later having drinks on board with Sam.

Do I have a good life or what? Given this easy itinerary, I decided to look up some details on our vodka swilling buddy, Andrei Pavnara. Room service arrived and they poured some coffee while I waited for Windows to boot. It took awhile – Windows, not pouring the coffee.

Lonnie came through our adjoining room door, looked at me and said, "I know what you're doing."

"Hey, wait. I'm the one who's supposed to be the 'Genius.' How could you know what I'm doing?"

"You're going to check on that Russian – or whatever he is – doctor."

Lonnie was right of course. Over breakfast, I did a few Google queries and made some notes in a small Notepad file that I kept open to record things that might be interesting. I proceeded to learn about Andrei Pavnara.

He was listed on the web site for Doctors Without Borders. His record showed that he was born in Russia in 1947. Apparently he liked warm weather because he attended the University of Havana as an undergraduate. After college, he was accepted into medical school at the Latin American Medical School, also in Havana.

His father, Vasili Pavnara, was a twenty-one year old up-and-coming naval officer when his son was born. I guess Pavnara senior was the equivalent of an Annapolis graduate. There was no information about Andrei's mother. The record indicated that Andrei Pavnara also attended high school in Havana.

I sat back and poured some more coffee. It seems odd, I thought, that Andrei would attend high school in Cuba. Assuming he began high school, like the rest of us, at age fourteen or fifteen, that would have been 1961 or 1962. So he went through high school during the Cuban Missile Crisis. Maybe his father knew something about the crisis that the rest of the world didn't.

If the father's career path went as expected, he would have been, by then, a Soviet naval officer.

"Wait, Lonnie, check this out. Vasili Pavnara was appointed Soviet Naval Attaché to Cuba in 1964. No wonder he traveled down here so often."

Lonnie grunted a neutral grunt. He grabbed his coffee and said, "So, our guy in the bar last night went from high school through med school; all here in Fidel's paradise. Interesting, I wonder why he wasn't educated back home in Mother Russia?"

"It has got to have something to do with the father."

"Yeah, maybe. But, if it does, why would a Soviet naval officer have his kid educated in Havana?"

"Maybe the father liked to visit his son to get away from Russia? I don't know. There could be lots of reasons."

"Hey, do you remember Andrei going on about the K-19 incident while you were ogling that blonde?"

"I wasn't ogling her. I was appreciating her beauty."

"Right!"

"Yeah, I remember the K-19 thing. Andrei claimed his father was an officer on the K-19; the nuclear sub with the bad cooling system."

"Well, let's check out the father."

"Later, we'll do that later. Right now we are tourists in Cuba, so let's go touring."

***

Since we were tourists, we did tourist things. We walked around Mariel checking out boats, marinas and other tourists. There were huge container ships constantly moving in and out of the harbor. Fishing boats fought their way through a maze of obstacles in order to bring their product to market.

Finally, to be dubbed official tourists, we bought tickets on an actual tour boat named the *Mariel Maiden*. The *Mariel Maiden* was a sizable craft – holding a limit of forty-five passengers and crew. It was equipped with two two hundred-fifty horsepower engines that could put some speed on the vessel if necessary. The *Maiden* had a hull made of what appeared to be steel grates with attached gate latches.

The gates, when deployed, lowered and raised themselves, serving as exit and entry points for the passengers. Pretty good design for a tourist boat.

It's an entirely different perspective when you are a passenger aboard a boat rather than a crew member responsible for specific duties.

So off we went; next to people, who wore sandals with black socks, island-themed flowered shirts and fanny packs. The tour boat crew set up a bar and turned on the music – Jimmy Buffet, of course. I was starting to like this tour boat thing. A few couples asked if I would take their picture while they waved rum drinks in the air. They had their arms around each other and were captured by their adventure out on the sea. Lonnie just rolled his eyes and turned away.

When people asked me what I was doing in Cuba, I always answered, "I'm a doctor here for a medical conference in Havana." I was pretty safe with that one. If they asked what kind of doctor, I would say that I was an internist. That's as deep as I went by way of explanations.

I thoroughly enjoyed being motored around the waterfront. There were cruise ships, container ships, commercial fishing vessels and other tour boats all competing for their space on the sea. The first mate on the *Mariel Maiden* told me that this is normal traffic for Mariel. He also told me that they had a pretty wild booze cruise departing right before sunset each day. I took a sideways glance at the mate. He looked at me and said, "Check it out, Senor."

Mariel is a beautiful city located in the Artemisia Province of Cuba. It is about thirty miles west of the city of Havana. There is a large deep water harbor that is getting deeper by the day due to extensive dredging by international investors – like the Chinese.

Of course, our embargo prevents the United States from participating in any economic ventures with the evil Cuban communist regime. The Cuban Government has established a special economic development zone that is a primary part of the city's growing trade activity.

Mariel Harbor can accommodate deeper draft vessels than the Port of Havana can. The Port of Havana can no longer be expanded because of an automobile tunnel that gets in the way.

Chapter 18

Late that afternoon we made our way back to *Epithelia* and met up with Sam. Over drinks he told us how receptive the Cuban medical community was to his practical experience with burn victims.

He also had the opportunity to interact with some of his colleagues from Doctors Without Borders. Lonnie asked him, "Sam, did you ever meet a Russian doctor named Pivnada or Pavnara? How the hell do you pronounce his name, Johnny?"

"It's Pavnara, Andrei Pavnara," I said. Sam replied, "Oh, Andy, yeah we met a few years back. We've spent time comparing research at different Doctors Without Borders conferences. I couldn't say he was a close friend but he definitely is in the friend category. I've listened to him rant before. Why? Do you know 'Heavy Handed Andy'?"

I answered, "Well, we spent some time together at our hotel bar last night." Lonnie said, "It was more like he talked and we listened."

"That's 'business as usual' for Andy. Did he get into the submarine thing about his father being a Soviet Naval Lieutenant on the K-19?"

"Yeah, he did. He appears to be passionate about the K-19. He seemed sincere and troubled as he spoke. He sounded quite believable."

"Oh he's 'the real deal' all right when it comes to nuclear subs, radiation sickness and serious skin restoration. If you catch him sober, he has some great stories. He also was an outstanding doctor, until the

Stolis got to him. He saved the lives of many Russian victims in the Chernobyl disaster. Chernobyl changed his life, just like the K-19 changed his father's life."

"Yeah, I can definitely understand that. So the thing with his father and the K-19 submarine incident is true?"

"Every word ... as Casey Stengel used to say, 'You can look it up'. In fact, the last time I saw him was about a year ago in Miami at a conference. He cornered me at the cocktail reception.

"He was going on about hidden nuclear materials and some kind of KGB plot involving Jack Kennedy, and then there was the radiation sickness. I don't know. He kept talking and rambling. The guy could go on. Believe me.

"At the Miami conference, he gave me a CD that he said contained all of his research on his father as well as modern-day patient records. Andy was obsessed with this stuff.

"My guess is he didn't have anyone else to give it to. I never did look at the files on that CD. I have about five or six CDs in my briefcase. Each CD is labeled 'Medical Research' with a subtitle like 'Burn Victims' or 'Case Studies.'

"The briefcase is in my hotel room with the rest of my stuff. I didn't give it much thought actually. I think the one Andy gave me is labeled 'Case Studies'.

"Why? Are you two going to research the K-19 disaster or are you just curious about Stolichnaya? Hey, I gotta go. I have a Doctors Without Borders dinner in Havana to get to. Maybe I'll see Andy there? I'll look for you guys later at your hotel bar."

With that, Sam climbed off the boat to shore
side. He looked down at me and said, "Johnny, if you
want to know about all that crazy stuff Andy was
blabbering about, talk to the old bartender at your hotel.
Word has it that he knows everything about everything
that has gone on in Mariel." He waved to us and took a
taxi back to his hotel, leaving Lonnie and me to stare
off into the harbor. I think I mentioned that I spend a
good deal of my life staring. After a short while, Lonnie
went below and started up his laptop. This time we
looked into Vasili Pavnara.

***

After awhile, Lonnie looked up from his screen
and said, "Check it out. Vasili Pavnara was not only
involved in the K-19 accident in 1961 but was also in
the middle of the Cuban Missile Crisis in October 1962.
"He was a submarine group commander. It
looks like he was the senior officer of four diesel
powered subs that were headed towards Cuba. They
were to escort Soviet ships intending to deliver nuclear
weapons to that island. Pavnara's submarine, the B-59,
carried its own nuclear missiles..."
I sipped my beer and thought about the B-59
cruising around the Florida Straits in a standoff with
disaster. The Crisis came to a head on October 27,
1962. On that day Pavnara, who was a young man, only
thirty-six yeas of age, had to make one of the most
important decisions in history.
The aircraft carrier USS Randolph detected the
B-59 near Cuba. The US vessel began dropping training

depth charges in an attempt to force the submarine to the surface for positive identification.

The US Navy repeatedly sent messages that practice depth charges were being used. These messages never reached the B-59 or Soviet Naval Headquarters.

The B-59 had not had contact with Moscow for several days. The Soviets actually got their information from tuning in to Miami based news broadcasts. In addition, the US was unaware that the Soviet sub was carrying nuclear weapons … so it kept pummeling the sub with these practice depth charges. Something had to give! The B-59 carried nuclear tipped torpedoes. These torpedoes could conceivably bring down the USS Randolph and force the beginning of a nuclear war.

If that had happened, the nuclear clouds would have spread from sea to land as the horror of nuclear war made its way across the globe. The first targets would have been Moscow, London and Berlin.

As that day wore on, the Crisis edged us closer and closer to war. That was when Soviet Naval Regulations came into play. There were three primary officers on board the B-59. One of them was Pavnara. It looked like from what we were reading on the screen, that he was top dog. He was equal in rank to the ship's captain but second-in-command of the B-59 itself, while also being the flotilla commander… confusing to say the least.

Next in line for the B-59 throne, as I understood it, was the political officer. The captain was authorized to launch a nuclear tipped torpedo only if all three agreed unanimously to do so. The B-59 was the only sub in the flotilla that required three officers to authorize the launch of a nuke. The other three subs only required the captain and the political officer to approve the launch. Maybe they didn't have nukes on that day? I don't know. No wonder the damn Soviet empire went to hell – *political officers*!

I got up from my seat and opened two Heinekens. I handed one to Lonnie. He grunted an approval grunt. We sat in silence absorbing what we read.

The B-59 captain, Valentin Savitsky, believed that a nuclear war had begun. There was no direction from Moscow. There was no communication with Moscow.

The sub needed to surface as temperatures inside reached over one hundred twenty degrees. The sub's batteries were in desperate need of recharging. Otherwise, their systems would begin to fail, one by one. The only way to save the sub and its crew was to surface.

The captain demanded that they fire the nuclear torpedo and get on with World War III. He asked for a consensus from the other two ranking officers. Vasili Pavnara refused! Images of the K-19 stormed his memory. He had visions of young sailors with their skin peeling off. He just could not unleash that horror to untold millions of innocent people. He steadfastly refused to fire a nuclear torpedo and did so while under tremendous pressure from the other two officers.

Valentin Savitsky wanted to launch a nuclear torpedo into the USS Randolph, the huge aircraft carrier leading the US task force. Savitsky, who proved to be exhausted both physically and mentally, assumed that his submarine was doomed and that World War III had begun. He ordered the B-59's ten kiloton nuclear torpedo to be prepared for launch. Its target was the USS Randolph, the giant aircraft carrier leading the task force.

The deadly torpedo was moved into the launch bay and awaited its next command. The world stood poised on the brink of oblivion. Pavnara wouldn't budge from his position. Regardless of the chiding of the political officer and the screaming of the captain, Pavnara stood his ground.

Had that torpedo been launched, it would have initiated a nuclear war with the Soviet Union and quickly have cascaded into a global conflict – killing untold millions of people.

The heroic actions of Vasili Pavnara forced the B-59 to surface since her batteries had to be charged. After some heated words in the control room, the B-59 turned and headed back to Russia. The Cuban Missile Crisis was effectively over.

Years later Defense Secretary Robert McNamara said, "In the end, it was luck. We were this close to nuclear war, and luck prevented it."

It is amazing, when you dig deeper into the Crisis, how much luck changed the decision making equation on that day. What if Pavnara went ahead with the decision to launch the nukes? What if the other two officers decided to launch anyway? What if one of the other three Soviet subs launched a missile? What if JFK decided his nation was in peril and gave the order to launch ... The list goes on.

Ultimately, Pavnara would be brought down in disgrace by his own people. Instead of applauding Pavnara, he was branded as a coward – someone who backed down to Kennedy – someone who embarrassed the Soviet Submarine Service – someone who was put under watch by the KGB

So, as fate would have it, the decision to prevent the two strongest military powers in the world from decimating the planet was made in the sweaty control room of a submarine by a thirty-six year old officer whom most people have never heard of. How did things get so out of control?

Sandy Mason

December 1961 - The United States of America

Us Intelligence Detects Soviet Submarine Activity In The Florida Straits.

East Germany Finishes Building The Berlin Wall To Halt The Flood Of Refugees Into The West.

USSR Detonates A Fifty Megaton Hydrogen Bomb In The Largest Man-Made Explosion In History.

There Are More Than 2,000 US Military Advisers In South Vietnam.

The US Continues Its Manned Space Program.

President Kennedy Is Named Time Magazine's '1961 Man Of The Year'.

Chrysler Corporation Introduces The Dodge Dart.

*The New York Mets Prepare For Their Inaugural Season In 1962.
They Would Lose One Hundred Twenty Games That Year.*

Chapter 19

All of this submarine warfare stuff was tiring. I was long overdue for a nap. Besides, I needed to think about something other than Russian submarines that were long since put out to pasture. So I settled in and thought about women.

I missed Carmen tremendously. Her Bahamian accent and flashing green eyed smile stayed with me. I hadn't seen her since I was back home in Bradenton. I had been gallivanting around Florida and the Bahamas for well over a year now.

Sometimes I was alone on these trips and sometimes I wasn't. That's just the way things worked for me. Look, how the hell was I going to manage a steady relationship on that kind of a schedule? I am such an asshole! I am one hundred percent asshole! No, I am a one hundred and ten percent asshole!

For god's sake, I'm over fifty years old. I should have a steady woman in the picture. As for Carmen, our last time together, sitting on the dock, trying to sort things out, was filled with awkward silences and thinly veiled criticisms. It raised more questions than answers.

Women seem to have not only a sixth sense but also a seventh, eighth and ninth sense about their relationships with me. They just see things that I don't see. They dance around a topic like a hurricane deciding on a place to make landfall. Me, I just go about my business and nail up the storm shutters. Then, I wait for the weather to settle and take them back down again! What's so tough about that? Well, according to one of these senses, to begin with, I should have put up the shutters a long time ago and I should have an immediate plan for the next emergency. Apparently I need to do this instead of kicking back and watching the ball game.

There are a lot of storms in this life. I don't spend an inordinate amount of time thinking about them. I just know they are out there. I know how to steer a boat directly into the wind so that you have some control and can minimize damage.

Carmen ran smack dab into a storm that involved my former girlfriend, Jane. She didn't have any control. It was either Carmen's eighth sense or Jane's ninth sense – we'll never know – that sent me walking. I had the distinction of making them both, simultaneously, unhappy.

Now, as far as Carla goes, she couldn't be more perfect for my so-called life style. She made no demands on me and would rather watch a good storm come in while holding a glass of dark rum. I believe she shares my storm shutter philosophy. We have spent several months together now and no big storms have yet to cross our bow.

***

I awoke to the sound of reggae music coming from the thatched roof bar at the edge of the marina. I took a quick boat shower and put on fresh jeans. Next I dug up a New York Yankees tee shirt and cap. Fidel would not have approved of this outfit but it didn't seem to ruffle anyone's feathers at happy hour. In fact, I got several high fives from the small but growing thatched roof crowd. We had a lightweight dinner and some Cuba Libres – just to be friends with the locals. A Cuba Libre is much more than a rum and coke with a lime added to it … It stands for 'Free *Cuba.*' It is a drink with attitude served in a side-car. It has a history that dates back to the Spanish American War.

We talked to a few locals who pointed to my Yankee hat. Baseball is very big in Cuba. One guy gave us the names of Cuban players to watch. Everyone spoke mostly English with a few switching back and forth to Spanish.

We decided to make it an early night when a man approached our table. He looked about fifty-five or sixty years old, tall and fit with an engaging smile. He looked at me as if he knew me, extended his hand and said, "Senor Donohue, I am Ernesto Clemente."

Before Lonnie and I left for Cuba, Carla had asked me to find out what we could about her brother's situation. On one of the secretive phone calls to her brother, she gave him the information on the Doctors Without Borders party, including our vessel name and location. It seems Ernesto found me before I found him.

Ernesto began the conversation, "My sister speaks highly of you, Senor Donohue."

"Please call me Johnny. This is my good friend …"

"Lonnie Turner," Ernesto broke in and he and Lonnie shook hands.

We spoke for awhile using 'couched' language – after all, the guy was wanted for killing a Cuban Naval officer. He was working as a mate on a tour boat right there in Mariel. Could this be the mate I spoke to briefly earlier today? Visitors to Cuba took ecology tours and sunset cruises as part of their hotel package. Ernesto catered to that clientele. He told us that his tour boat was the *Mariel Maiden*. He asked me to email Carla and let her know that we had made contact. We talked for a short while and agreed to meet for dinner the following night.

Cuban Exile

Chapter 20

Lonnie and I took a leisurely stroll through the marina section and back to our hotel. We passed by the scene of last night's world history vodka lesson. I just had to take a peek in. I did huge double-take when I saw that Andrei Pavnara had Sam pushed into a corner at the end of the bar. It did not look at all as if Sam wanted to be there.

Lonnie immediately sized up the situation. He walked into the bar and shoved his six-foot three frame in between the two men. Pavnara got the idea and backed away.

He must have been hitting the Stolis a bit too hard because he was rambling on to Sam about what the Soviets did to his father and why his father should be admired as a national hero. Then he went on about the KGB and President Kennedy and finished off his little diatribe with something about radiation sickness, geographic coordinates and imminent danger.

I walked over to the bartender, the same guy we had last night. The guy that Sam told us about. I indicated that 'Heavy Handed Andy' had had enough for tonight. He nodded at me and made the same circular motion with his hand that he had made the night before.

I walked back to the corner of the bar. Sam grabbed my forearm. "Johnny, can you get him out of here and back up to his room? I don't know what the hell he is talking about with respect to these geographic coordinates. He's supposed to deliver a paper tomorrow. I know he's a mess tonight but there was a time when he was a leading surgeon in his field. I feel as though I'm responsible for him."

"Yeah well, I hope the coordinates will help him to get there if he remembers to show up." I looked at Andy, "Hey buddy, you need to call it a night. It's time to go. Say good night Irene, sayonara Susie, arrivederci Alice, you get the idea. Here, let me give you a hand up the stairs."

"I'm not going anywhere," he said. Lonnie looked at him with a no-nonsense face and placed one of his arms around Andy's waist and with the other grabbed him by the wrist and pulled him up and out of the bar stool. Then he walked or, should I say, pulled Andy up the one flight of stairs to his room.

His room was only three or four doors down the landing from where we were staying. He led Andrei to his doorway and watched as he fumbled for his key.

Pavnara finally found the room key and Lonnie unlocked the door for him. He pointed Pavnara in the direction of the bed. It was lights out for 'Heavy Handed Andy' and his conspiracy lectures. Lonnie left and closed the door behind him.

I paid the bar bill and couldn't help but notice the same blonde sitting alone at her table way in the back. Maybe it's her favorite spot?

After the Pavnara scene, Sam took off and headed back to his own hotel. The conference was scheduled to last another two days and he had lots of work to do.

Lonnie walked back down the single flight of stairs and into the bar area. Things were a lot calmer after dropping off the partially comatose Andrei Pavnara.

Cuban Exile

We both absorbed the evening. The bar was eerily quiet after our little scuffle. The night air was dripping with heat and humidity. A Spanish guitar played softly on the veranda. In the distance, luxury yachts announced their presence with two blasts on their marine horns.

Cuba had its own aura – its own rhythm – its own pace – its own moods. It feels different from the Bahamas or Jamaica or Puerto Rico. I don't know why. It just does. A feeling can be hard to describe but, whatever it is, Cuba has one. The people are wonderful … the government – that was another thing.

Tomorrow would be the time to think about what we needed to do to get the boat back to the States. I would email Carla about Ernesto and see about availability of slips in Key West while doing some electronic flirting at the same time. I am a true multi-tasking guy. You can ask any of my managers when I did my sentence in corporate. I could go to a long lunch and then leave early all in the same day!

At any rate, we needed the obvious grocery shopping as well as a check of all the systems on board the boat – same old stuff we always do. I fell asleep thinking of the way Carla looked when she walked down the dock.

Chapter 21

Andrei Pavnara's body was found by the hotel staff shortly after 10 AM on Wednesday March 17, 2010. That morning he was supposed to be delivering a paper on the treatment of radiation sickness victims.

Instead, he was lying face down in his bed. There were two nine millimeter slugs in the back of his head – an execution style murder. Andrei Pavnara had told his last tale.

Andrei was found fully clothed in his trademark beige linen suit. His shoes were still on and so was his tie. It appeared as though someone had lie in wait for him. That person wasted no time.

As soon as Pavnara entered the room he probably fell face first onto the mattress and passed out. All the shooter needed to do was to open the door, walk over to the bed and squeeze off two rounds into Pavnara. Then the shooter would step back, peer out at the landing and wait for the right moment to slip away.

It was a simple yet elegant way of getting rid of someone. There was no elevator, only a simple two-level hotel with a single staircase – easy to slip by unnoticed.

***

News of Andrei Pavnara's murder spread quickly. By mid-afternoon it seemed everyone who was anyone was aware that there had been a murder in the

Cuban Exile

Mariel Hotel. The Mariel Marine Police were already investigating. There were people on the dock standing around in little groups pointing and gesturing. Each offering an opinion. Doctors Without Borders cancelled the remaining two days of the conference. It seems everyone was in the know - everyone except Lonnie and me.

We were as clueless as a newborn baby as to what all the excitement was about. As planned, Lonnie and I got up early, checked out of the hotel and headed out on boat errands. I was at the ship's store and Lonnie was in and out of a few places finding what he needed. We stopped for coffee and started planning our way back to Key West.

In the background I could see police cars pull into the marina area. They had loud, whiny sirens. We finished our coffee and headed back to *Epithelia*. As we got closer, it became obvious that several police officers were hovering around our boat.

Entry to the boat was blocked by cops. I could see two officers on board looking through our belongings. I yelled over to them, "Hey, what the hell …" I was cut off by a voice behind me; my old buddy *Marine Police Commander Whitesuit.*

There he stood straight as the arrow that must have been shoved up his ass earlier that day. He was decorated to the nines. His white uniform was dripping with medals and he was surrounded by his minions. I counted eight uniformed cops.

"Senor Donohue, Senor Turner, come with me please. You are wanted for questioning concerning the death of Andrei Pavnara." With that he put both of his hands on my chest and pushed me back towards the uniformed goons.

I was getting very pissed off at this guy. He was being a prick in light of our little altercation when we first landed in Mariel.

"Hey, what the hell is this all about?" Before I could get that sentence out, one of the uniforms took out his baton and showed it to me. He poked me in the stomach with the butt of the stick – not too hard, not too soft. I got the message. I looked at Lonnie, who evaluated the situation and said, "Do as he says."

"Your friend, Senor Turner, is very wise."

"Yeah, how would you recognize anyone who is wise?" I got another poke – this one was harder and into my ribs. I stumbled backwards absorbing the pain.

Lonnie called over to me. "Just shut up and do what he says." This time Whitesuit had one of his charges take the shopping bags from my hand. Another goon took Lonnie's stuff. The packages disappeared to who knows where as I was frisked and then pushed into the back of a police cruiser. As the car took off, I thought I saw Ernesto Clemente in the crowd.

Lonnie was also frisked and shoved into a second car. We were both whisked away to a very old concrete building where we stopped and got out of the cars. The cops forced us inside. We were pushed forward and directed by night stick into adjoining cells – just like the Mariel Hotel. Anyway you looked at it …

Johnny Donohue and Lonnie Turner were *in jail!*

Chapter 22

I sat on the concrete bench that the Cubans had generously provided and took in my jail cell. It really wasn't much to look at. Well, there was the concrete bench, a small bathroom enclosed by concrete and a sink that dripped out water lined with rust.

Given the water pressure in the sink, it would take an hour to wash your hands, that is, if you had soap. There was no soap, no towels, and no windows. Neither one of us could stand up straight in the cell. I think it was designed by leftover torturers from the Spanish Inquisition.

We sat on the concrete benches – staring out in front of us. There was a large iron door that led to somewhere we had yet to be led. Lonnie did not say what I thought he would say, that was, *"If you had kept your goddamn mouth shut we wouldn't be in this Hilton."* Instead he just grunted at me and said, "Freakin Genius."

Being in jail in a foreign country that is classified as a third world country, is unnerving. Essentially, you have no civil rights – no platform to complain into – nothing between you and the police and whatever semblance of a judicial system that country allows. This was the situation in which we found ourselves.

***

Law enforcement in Cuba is the responsibility of the *Policía Nacional Revolucionaria*, the PNR -- sounds like a nice bunch of guys. The PNR is controlled by the Cuban Ministry of the Interior. This is where opportunity abounds for young Cubans. As any loyal citizen knows, the Cuban Constitution states that "Defense of the socialist motherland is every Cuban's greatest honor and highest duty."

In order to achieve this greatest honor and highest duty, you are conscripted into either the armed forces or the PNR. The draft is compulsory for all those over the age of sixteen. However, conscripts have no choice as to which organization they are assigned. So it's boda bing -- bada boom – out of high school and into the army or maybe the police. No further discussion required.

We were arrested by the police so I assumed we were under control of the PNR. The maze of government organizations within the PNR eventually leads to the office of *Internal Order and Crime Prevention.* There is an entire substructure of government that continues down that wandering lane but you get the idea ... more government, more bureaucracy, more offices.

Cuba has fourteen provinces, each of which has its own Police Chief. The Police Chief reports to a central PNR command in Havana.

What I was soon to find out was that Mr. Whitesuit was in fact, Miquel Cabrara, Police Chief of Mariel Province. He was also known as Shore-Side Naval Commander. Both the shore-side police as well as the Harbor Police were at his disposal. I had pissed off the wrong guy!

***

Miquel Cabrara was born in 1950, about ten years prior to Fidel's revolution. His father was a career policeman who quickly disowned the Batista regime in 1960 and pledged his loyalty to Fidel and the Communist paradise that became Cuba.

Like his father, Miquel spent his career in law enforcement – at least Fidel's brand of law enforcement. At age sixteen, he was conscripted into the Cuban service as were all sixteen year olds. When he graduated from high school, he trained to be a cop and made up his mind to spend his career in law enforcement.

Higher ranking police officials are drawn from police schools and college programs. Cabrara studied police science in college and then moved on to the police academy. There he had the opportunity to become an officer. It was his dream to become a lieutenant and then move up to captain. He continued his college education and continued to climb up the police ladder.

As Cabrara's career advanced, so to did the power of the PNR. The PNR now has a wide range of police cars spread throughout the major cities of Cuba.

This I witnessed first hand as Lonnie and I were taken away in two separate patrol cars -- Peugeots for God's sake! Who the hell uses Peugeots for police cars?

Sandy Mason

The PNR has grown to the point that it has become a significant presence in the everyday lives of the Cuban people. The police regularly patrol on foot and use radio communications, as well as a computer dispatching system. PNR officers are armed with a semi-automatic handgun and a baton. These they may use if necessary to apprehend suspects and to defend themselves.

Miquel Cabrara's career advancement folded nicely into the expanding powers of the NRP. By age twenty-six, he rose to the rank of lieutenant and then several years later became a captain. Cabrara kept himself physically fit, never smoked, drank occasionally and was enough of a politician to maneuver his way to the position of Chief of Police.

Cabrara had a history of physical abuse towards his prisoners. There were reports that Cabrara himself participated in the much rumored 'death squads' of the nineteen seventies. Thus began his long and beautiful friendship with the Security Police. As a young officer, he supposedly beat several suspects to death at the bequest of the Security Police.

These actions cemented his relationship with the Cuban Security Police. Cabrara's troopers were virtually at the beck and call of the Security Police. This enabled the detectives of the Security Police to dig deeper into their suspects. They easily moved through any layer of citizen resistance to get to their goal knowing they were backed up by an endless supply of muscle.

At any rate, they had all the power and I had none. That's just the way things were!

Cuban Exile

***

Sleeping on a concrete bench has a way of taking the piss and vinegar out of a person. It removes the sarcasm and sense of humor that some people carry around and replaces them with anger and resentment.

I dozed on and off while curled up on the bench. I had no idea whether it was day or night since there were no windows in our cells. Our watches were taken. Our pockets were emptied and our cash and credit cards had disappeared. Neither of us knew why or how Andrei Pavnara got himself dead.

Looking at our situation – only Sam knew that we had checked out of our hotel and were supposed to be staying on *Epithelia* in the marina. But Sam may have been tied up with the authorities as well as with Doctors Without Borders.

He could be busy with paperwork, notification of family members and who knows what? He might even be in jail himself. It was a homicide, for God's sake. He could be undergoing interrogation in some rat hole like the one we were in. He wouldn't go looking for us until he finished up with police business, checked out of his hotel and headed to the marina. That could be hours – maybe even days.

Today was the day we were supposed to load up the boat and prepare to leave Cuba. Well, we sure missed the channel marker on that one. I thought about last night -- before we ran into the mad Russian. The only person we spoke to was Ernesto Clemente, who also may have been present during my arrest. We made a dinner date and went our separate ways. The next day we were in jail! How did everything get so screwed up?

Sandy Mason

May 1962 The United States of America

Astronaut Scott Carpenter orbits the Earth and overshoots landing zone by 250 miles.

The first nuclear explosion to be caused by an American ballistic missile is accomplished at Christmas Island, 1,200 miles from its launch site.

Officials of the CIA meet with US Attorney General Robert F. Kennedy and implore him to stop the investigation of Mafia crime boss Sam Giancana.

The Beatles sign their first recording contract, with Parlophone.

Marilyn Monroe makes her last significant public appearance, singing "Happy Birthday, Mr. President" at a birthday party for President Kennedy. Monroe was stitched into a $12,000 dress "made of nothing but beads" and wore nothing underneath.

Soviet leader Nikita Khrushchev accepted the recommendation from his Defense Council, to place nuclear missiles in Cuba.

Lee Harvey Oswald arrives in Moscow.

The first James Bond movie - 'Dr. No' was released.

New York Yankee Center Fielder Mickey Mantle leads the American League in hitting.

Chapter 23

So there I sat – along with my now-hostile best friend, Lonnie, in a building made out of concrete blocks. The temperature was rising. Sweat dripped off of my face. My shirt smelled like leftover tuna fish. I took it off and threw it in the corner of the cell. It was a New York Yankees tee shirt but I just couldn't take it anymore.

After what seemed to me to be a block of time that was longer than a sixteen inning baseball game - the iron door opened. Two uniformed guards came into the cell corridor after rapidly closing the iron door behind them. They brought each of us two plastic twelve-ounce bottles of water. They also brought some kind of sandwich that I couldn't recognize. I would have given my entire jacket collection for a single Heineken...

I yelled at the guards, "Hey, we are Americans. I demand to be taken to our authorities. Get it, comrades?" They just laughed at me. I elevated the conversation and told them something to the effect that they could contact their mothers over at the Red Light District.

I expected Lonnie to yell at me for being so brash with the prison guards, but he didn't. He had had it with this *Jailhouse Rock* routine and was ready to bust these guys up. Our frustration levels had reached the point where our anger had surfaced unbridled – ready for a fight. We were in a desperate situation. The *Bill of Rights* had yet to make its way to Cuba. Is

America really only ninety miles from this island paradise?

I still couldn't make any sense of the fact that Andrei Pavnara spilled his guts to us about his father and events from over fifty years ago. Maybe there was something he was leading up to in his rage - something from the present day, but why tell me and Lonnie? I mean, KGB plots to kill Jack Kennedy, radiation sickness. I don't know.

Pavnara was supposed to be an expert in radiation sickness but is there radiation sickness running around Cuba that we don't know about? Pavnara lived here in Cuba. Why would anyone kill a radiation sickness specialist?

Maybe there was more to be told on the CD that he passed off to Sam? Our only hope of getting out of here lay with Doctor Sam Feldman. I could only hope that he could pull off an escape or a release of some type.

I thought about tying the bed sheets together and lowering myself out the window and then down the side of the building. Of course, there were no bed sheets and there was no window – so that plan fell apart!

My mind was racing away from logical thought and entering the realm of the mysterious. In an effort to initiate a conversation, I asked Lonnie, "So, what were the different plots to kill JFK that have surfaced after all these years?"

"Jeeze, there's lots of them. The usual suspects include the CIA, the Mafia, Castro himself, the KGB, Oswald alone, anti-Castro Cubans. The list seems to grow each year."

"Do you remember where Kennedy was right before he went to Texas?"

"Yeah, like it was yesterday man. He was in Tampa less than a week or so before the assassination.

"It was the biggest thing ever to hit Tampa. My father took me out of school for the day. It was a pretty big deal. No sitting President had ever visited Tampa.

"We stood on the sideline of a passing parade. There he was, larger than life, a good-looking guy, smiling, waving to the crowds of people that lined the streets; standing up in an open convertible. I remember that it was a Lincoln. It also was the same convertible that he rode in on his trip through Dallas some five days later."

"Whoa, so you really saw him?"

"Yeah, I did and I never forgot it."

Lonnie went on to tell me a little about Tampa's leading Mafioso, Santo Trafficante, Jr. Trafficante has always been suspected of having a hand in murdering JFK. Trafficante hated the Kennedys because of Bobby Kennedy's vendetta against organized crime. Trafficante and Chicago mobster, Sam Giancana, have long been suspected of plotting to kill the President but as usual there is no direct proof.

To make things even more uncertain, Trafficante was working both sides of the street. He conspired with various CIA operatives and was involved in several unsuccessful plans to assassinate Castro. This much was confirmed by the CIA's 2007 declassification of the "Family Jewels" documents.

Giancana and Trafficante 'stayed in touch' - each presiding over his criminal organizations in

Chicago and Tampa… each with his own reasons for killing JFK.

This is where Frank Sinatra came into play. Frank served as a go-between for Giancana and Bobby Kennedy. Giancana had allegedly helped JFK win the state of Illinois by means that may be considered questionable.

Now the mobster was furious with the President for giving his brother free reign over prosecuting high level mob criminals. In particular, Bobby had Giancana's home under surveillance twenty-four hours a day. Giancana absolutely hated JFK!

Just when you thought you've heard it all, Jack Kennedy and Sam Giancana actually shared the same woman, Judith Cambell, on and off for a period of time. Throw in their mutual hatred of Castro and you've got yourself quite a mixed drink!

Years later in 1975, Giancana was called to testify before a United States Senate Committee investigating Mafia involvement in a failed CIA plot to assassinate Castro. He was shot and killed two days before he was to testify. This particular shooting took on special meaning. Giancana had been shot once in the back of the head and then for good measure -- six times in a neatly stitched circle around the mouth. It was the Mafia's way of warning others to keep their mouths shut.

Some suspected that Trafficante had ordered the hit. There are plenty of theories as to who killed him …rival Mafiosi, CIA operatives, one of his former girlfriends, Fidel Castro. Who knows? No one was ever arrested in connection with the murder.

Cuban Exile

Trafficante was unfazed by Giancana's murder. He went on his merry way in Tampa – opening strip clubs – supporting gambling operations and getting involved in smuggling of all sorts – drugs, weapons – you name it. When the topic of JFK came up, Trafficante seemed to hide behind the thin veil of truth that surrounded the assassination.

Less than two years later, in 1977, Trafficante was himself served with a subpoena to testify before the House Assassinations Committee. The questions put to him were as frank and direct as possible. He was asked if he had anything to do with the death of Jack Kennedy. Did he ever discuss any plans to assassinate President Kennedy? Did he know Jack Ruby? Did he know Lee Harvey Oswald? Trafficante took the fifth on every question he was asked.

Chapter 24

It seemed that another half day or so had passed while we sat on our concrete benches. My two bottles of water were long gone. I was prepared to apologize to the guards for commenting on their matriarchal heredity if I could get two more. That didn't happen.

Before we left Key West I did some reading about Americans who have sailed to Cuba. Officially, we were not supposed to visit Cuba – but no one bothered you if you did. Americans brought in cash and cash is what Cubans needed. Marinas, restaurants, hotels, charter boats and who knows what were benefitting from greenbacks. Unofficially, Americans were welcomed by the Cuban people.

As far as diplomatic relations were concerned, we had not had an embassy in Cuba since 1961. Political issues between the American Government and the Cuban Government were handled by the Swiss Embassy, specifically *by 'The United States Interests Section of the Embassy of Switzerland'* or as government officials would say - USINT Havana. The Swiss have made a fortune mediating disputes between hostile governments – and all this time I thought they just climbed mountains, yodeled and drank hot chocolate.

So what I needed was a USINT person or a guy from Switzerland wearing a traditional red vest. He doesn't necessarily have to be the Section Chief of USINT – just someone to get me out of this goddamn place. In fact, I didn't really care what he wore as long as I could finish up with Cabrara and his flunkies and sail the hell out of here.

Marinas in Cuba have scores of American vessels of all shapes and sizes docked there – including some mega yachts. The American Government is acutely aware of this. USINT constantly updates Washington DC as to goings on in Cuban ports.

Now, on the other side of the political landscape, lies the USINT counterpart. That would be the *Interests Section of the Republic of Cuba in Washington*.

Switzerland also handles the Cuban side of things. It's kind of like allowing your wife's lawyer to handle the divorce procedure for both of you. I wondered if these INT people ever went to happy hour together.

I told Lonnie my thoughts on Switzerland and the INT people. He was not amused. He said, "Look, we have to get to Sam or Sam has to get to us. It's that simple. Otherwise we might rot to death in this hole."

The thought that Sam might be in jail himself or that he might be going through the 'questioning' phase of his arrest scared me. Actually, we didn't know squat about anything beyond this cell.

A few hours later the iron door clinked open. Two armed guards approached us. Again they gave us two bottles of water each and two strange looking sandwiches. I drank the first bottle of water like there was no tomorrow. Lonnie addressed one of the guards with a firm but even tone. "Tell your boss that I am a retired cop from Washington DC. People will be looking for me."

"You can tell him yourself Senor. The Chief of Police will see you shortly."

"The Chief?" The guards started to leave for their sanctuary behind the iron door.

"Wait," Lonnie said to one of the guards. "Is he the one in the white uniform?"

"Si Senor, Police Chief Miquel Cabrara. He will see you when he is ready."

Lonnie looked at me with a scowl. "Way to go, Genius. You managed to piss off the Police Chief on two separate occasions. Now we're walking into the interview with two strikes on us."

"Yeah, well, he could be more diplomatic when addressing Americans."

"He doesn't give a flying cannoli whether or not you're an American. We are in a foreign country. You got that? You have no rights. You have no due process. We are totally under their control."

"Yeah, yeah, yeah. I got all that. I'm still not going to knuckle under to these bastards."

"You know, there's a little Jack Kennedy in you."

"Too bad we don't have a PT boat."

Chapter 25

Later that day, Police Chief Miquel Cabrara had me transported to an air conditioned cell in a local police station. I had no shirt on. I wore sweaty jeans and a pair of now stinking boat shoes. I thought about all the nice clothes that I had on board the *Epithelia* ... Tommy Bahama shirts, Lacoste shorts and an endless supply of jackets.

I was badly in need of a shower. I was handcuffed behind my back and then chained to a fitting that was bolted into the floor. The chain ran through the frame of a rusting fold-up metal chair - the kind you see in a funeral parlor. Well, at least I had air conditioning.

A single uniformed guard preceded Cabrara's pompous entrance into the interrogation room. He kind of swept in -- like a woman in a gown making an entrance to a cocktail party. I tried to stand as a show of respect but the goon pushed me back down into the chair. I started to say something when Chief Cabrara interrupted me. "Silence! Do not speak until I tell you to." he shouted.

Great, another smooth, diplomatic standoff between me and Chief Whitesuit was now officially underway. I sat there in silence as Cabrara went through some papers in his briefcase. He pulled a few sheets out and made some notations. He looked up at me and said, "You may answer my questions now." Well, la dee fucking da, I get to answer his majesty's questions.

"Why did you kill Andrei Pavnara?" Well, there's nothing wrong with getting right to the point. I contained my usual sarcasm and answered. "I did not kill Andrei Pavnara."

"I have a witness who saw you on the hotel landing holding a gun on the night that Andrei Pavnara died."

"The only thing I was holding that night was a Stoli's on the rocks, compliments of Andrei Pavnara. Oh yeah, I had a lime wedge put in the drink."

"You were seen arguing with him on the night he was killed."

"On the night he died, Pavnara was arguing with anyone in sight – me included."

"Where is the gun you used to kill Andrei Pavnara?"

"I don't know what gun you are talking about. Look, I didn't kill Pavnara and I was unarmed at the hotel bar. Why would I kill a drunken doctor?"

"Do you own a gun, Senor?"

"Yeah, a thirty-eight caliber pistol, but you already know that because you probably ransacked my belongings and everything else on our boat – by the way, I could use a clean shirt."

"It is illegal to bring firearms into my country."

"Not if you are part of a sanctioned mission such as Doctors Without Borders. We were cleared upon entrance to Cuba by way of the Doctors Without Borders documents.

" Maybe you forgot that little tango we did at the dock?" Cabrara was fuming. "Do not tell me the laws of my country!" He stormed out of the room. The guard walked over to my chained-down chair and backslapped me hard across the face. I lunged at him but the son of a bitch moved out of range.

I sat in the chained up chair waiting for Cabrara's next move. About a half an hour or so later, he came back into the room. He carried two twelve ounce bottles of water. One he opened and practically drained on the spot. What water was left in the bottle he threw in my face. He put the second bottle on his desk. It was facing me just out of reach.

This whole session really was not going well. I was sure Lonnie would be getting these same questions. I was also sure that Lonnie would have been right ahead of me on the interview queue.

Cabrara began, "What did you and Pavnara talk about the night he was killed?" I regained my composure a few minutes after the water bottle attack.

"He was talking about his father being in the Russian Navy during the Missile Crisis."

"What else?"

"Well, he was rambling on about a number of topics. All of them seemed like ancient history to me."

"Topics like what?"

"Okay, he was going on about some kind of KGB plot involving Jack Kennedy and then there was the radiation sickness and nuclear submarines."

"Is that it?"

"Pretty much, oh yeah, something about geographic coordinates. I didn't understand a whole lot of what he was saying. The guy was bombed. He kept changing languages and my Russian is really bad. Do you speak Russian?" Cabrara smirked at me. "Look, Chief, why would I kill Pavnara? I knew him for forty-eight hours and during that time he drank enough vodka to sink a small battleship. Then he got himself dead." I paused a bit for dramatic effect before I said, "Hey, how about a clean shirt? "

"You smug bastard, I will get you a whole new outfit." With that he turned to the guard and said, "Sergeant, take him to booking."

The guard uncuffed me and motioned to the door. I yelled at Cabrara, "Hey, I am an American citizen. I want to see Sam Feldman and I want to speak to the USINT representative at the Swiss Embassy."

Cabrara just glared at me as I was led out of the interrogation room. I couldn't believe that that prick held me for all that time just to ask a few questions that he already knew the answers to. This was not over between us! Him and his pompous manner and that stupid clown suit he ran around in… asshole.

Chapter 26

Cabrara's sergeant had me fingerprinted along with the usual prison photo showing one's profile. Following that procedure, I was pushed into what looked like a supply room of some sort. A barely awake guard sat behind a counter. He and the laugh-a-minute sergeant exchanged some sort of joke that I'm sure was about me.

The supply guy threw an orange jumpsuit in my direction. Then he pulled out two bottles of water, a one quarter full roll of paper towels and a very used bar of soap. These items he tossed onto the counter in front of me.

They told me to put the jump suit on over my jeans. It smelled about as bad as the New York Yankees tee shirt I had thrown away. I was taken through a long hallway with about twenty jail cells that stood face to face, looking at each other. The sergeant pushed me into an empty cell, similar to the one I was placed in right after my arrest. I was back to no air conditioning again.

At that point I was totally depressed. There was no sign of Lonnie, no sign of Sam and no one at all who remotely looked like a USINT person or a guy from Switzerland. I was completely alone. I sat down on the concrete bench and sipped a bottle of water.

What the hell was this thing all about? Are the Cuban authorities bringing up something new about the Kennedy assassination? Do they think Andrei gave

Lonnie and me some secrets that would reveal earth shattering truths about JFK? How did a simple sailing trip turn into this nightmare of events?

***

Another day or so passed and I continued my diet of suspicious sandwiches and bottled water. I was about to start yelling for the guards to get me out of there when the steamy silence was broken.

I heard Lonnie's booming voice as the door at the end of the corridor opened. "You kept him in this rotted out dump because you wanted to interrogate him?" He said to no one but the jail guards who were following him. Never was I so glad to see Lonnie with his imposing six-foot-three build and determined stride.

One of the guards opened my cell and pushed the gate back. When I stepped out Lonnie gave me a bear hug. "Jeeeez, you smell like a dead fish."

"Yeah, they're not big on personal hygiene for prisoners around here. Even the guards stink." One of the guards took out his night stick, poked me and gestured for us to move down the corridor.

Lonnie glared at him and said, "You touch either of us with that stick again and I'll wrap it around your fuckin' neck!" There are times when you don't mess with Lonnie and this was one of them. Any language barrier that existed between him and the guards was quickly removed by the tone of his voice. As we walked to the prison interrogation room, other inmates watched in a jealous despair.

It was really no surprise to see Police Chief Miquel Cabrara waiting for us. To my delight, Sam was also there along with two other representatives of Doctors Without Borders. There was another guy present who looked like a civilian. I wasn't sure at all what his function was. Cabrara introduced him as Luis Ramirez, a member of the Cuban Security Police.

I told him that I had plenty of security and didn't need any more. He turned to Cabrara with a quizzical look. "Do not pay any attention to Senor Donohue. He thinks he is a comedian."

Sam opened up his briefcase and brought out papers from Doctors Without Borders indicating that Lonnie and I were on a mission of mercy for that entity and had in fact delivered medical supplies and provided logistical support to the conference that took place the previous week.

In addition, the papers stated that we were both American citizens with valid passports and posed no threat to the citizens of Cuba. In addition, we had cooperated with a criminal investigation. Any further questioning would be done only with our USINT representative from the Swiss Embassy.

The documents were signed by everyone in the room, including secret agent Ramirez. Ramirez stood about five-foot-six inches tall with a paunchy, lazy build and only wisps of hair. The hair stuck out in all crazy directions. It was hard to take him seriously as a secret agent, so I didn't.

Cabrara brought out his own set of papers. It was a real pissing contest conducted by big boys with legal documents. Cabrara's contribution to the paperwork carnival went on and on with clauses about the Swiss Embassy, contraband, marina fees, police incarceration fees, police administration fees and a whole bunch of stuff that I don't remember. The most important part of the documents stipulated that the *Epithelia* must remain in port under Cuban supervision as it was part of a criminal investigation.

Lonnie and I were ordered to stay in Mariel aboard the sailboat until such time as it was released to its rightful owner. Our passports would be returned to us when the Cuban Government deemed it proper.

Lonnie and I signed some paperwork that, in essence, kept us in Mariel until they had no further use for us. Sam had VIP status because he had valuable medical skills and because Doctors Without Borders would raise international holy hell if he was detained.

At that point, I would have signed my own death warrant just to get the hell out of there. I took off my orange jumpsuit and threw it in a corner of the room. I glared at Whitesuit and walked out into the blazing sunshine. I shielded my eyes for a long time before I attempted to move.

Chapter 27

Sam drove me to the marina but Lonnie stayed behind to talk to Cabrara and our newly-found friend, Ramirez. Hopefully, they were all getting along and talking cop-to-cop. As Cabrara and Ramirez left, Lonnie was chatting up one of the local street cops. He managed to bargain his way to the purchase of three thirty-eight caliber hand guns. Life was getting back to normal.

When I arrived at the boat, I took a shower, which drained the onboard water tank, then wrapped myself up in a towel and sat on the cabin bench with a cold Heineken in my hand.

I was drained. I drifted off to sleep thinking that I would never take my freedom for granted again. Those bastards locked me up in a box with sanitary conditions dating back to Batista's day. Cabrara would not get away with this. He had no idea who he was screwing with.

When I finally woke up and changed into civilized clothes, Sam, Lonnie and I began discussing our game plan. At that point, our game plan was that we had no game plan. I opened beers for everyone as we each found a comfortable spot in the air conditioned cabin. Sam began, "What do you think that 'Security Police' guy was all about?"

I had to hand it to Sam. In the space of a week or so, he had gone from being a world class surgeon to a sailboat navigator to standing up to a Cuban Police

Chief. In the wake of that, he deftly handled a murder investigation that led to getting his friends out of jail. I think this whole trip brought out elements of him that he never even knew he had.

I tried to answer Sam's question with my own set of questions. "This entire trip has been weird," I said. "Maybe we are overlooking something? Maybe we're looking in the wrong direction?

Why was Andrei Pavnara so anxious to tell us his father's sad story? Why was he killed? What was all that babble about JFK and finally; why is the Cuban Security Police interested in all this?"

The cabin got very quiet. Only the hum of the air conditioner could be heard. I continued, "Hey Sam, where is your briefcase? The one with all the CDs in it."

"It's here on board with my other stuff. I have three days before I have to be back in Tampa so I'm settling in here on the boat with you guys. Let me go get the CD."

Sam disappeared into his quarters and returned in a minute. "It looks like the Cubans went through my things but the briefcase is in tact. The CDs are all there, including the one Andy gave me - the one he labeled 'Case Studies'."

Lonnie and Sam both opened their laptops and started Goggling around. I opened up three more Heinekens and put them on the table. I also dug up something to eat from the galley while my troops set about solving the Pavnara mystery. I didn't actually have real food but at least it wasn't prison food – just frozen dinners to be micro waved, to be nuked, I thought. I yelled through the cabin, "Hey, anyone for a

110

nuclear dinner?" They just ignored me and continued their work while the microwave buzzed on.

***

A couple of hours and another round of drinks passed by with no new significant clues or hints or whatever we were looking for. Sam's 'Case Studies' CD held the latest data on Vasili Pavnara. Vasili made many trips between Russia and Havana – ostensibly to visit his son and to consult with both Cuban and Soviet Naval authorities. After all, at that time, he was Soviet Naval Attaché to Cuba. Lonnie and I were both reading the same screen and sharing the same thoughts.

I said, "Holding that position seems incongruous for an officer who had been disgraced. Maybe the disgrace routine was a phony, a setup of some kind. Maybe the attaché job was a vehicle for allowing free reign over Cuban Government activities. Maybe Vasili himself was KGB and this disgrace thing was all a ruse?"

Sam looked at us like a man on the verge of discovering something; something important but with words not yet fully formed. Finally he spoke, "Look at these notes that Andy made when he visited his father right before Vasili died back in 1998.

I guess I should have read the CD last year when he gave it to me. It's just that he was such a flake. I didn't know whether his rantings were just a bi-product of all the Stolichnaya he drank or the real McCoy. Now I believe that he was onto something."

"Yeah, something that got him very dead," I said.

Chapter 28

The next morning, over coffee, Lonnie and I sat in silence listening to Sam as he read from the somewhat cryptic notes that Andy left about meetings with his father, Vasili.

They were indirect notes, using no names – but important notes that may have led his son to discover that certain Soviet Admirals, who were KGB agents, planned to assassinate JFK.

It appeared that Vasili, for his own reasons, did not want any part of it. Maybe Vasili was again driven by the same motivation that caused him not to launch nuclear missiles back in 1962 – his fear of nuclear war.

Reading on, we may have hit the mother lode! Andrei's notes indicated that the assassination plan was to be executed in early1965, provided Kennedy won the 1964 election. I guess Lee Harvey Oswald was a runaway train and got to Kennedy long before the KGB did.

Still, you have to wonder if Vasili Pavnara knew more than he was giving up about the KGB - Kennedy assassination plot – if there was such a plot. I continued to probe the CD. I found a series of numbers that were buried deep inside Andrei's research section. I scribbled them onto a sheet of paper and passed them off to Lonnie.

They read … 55.55   23.13   27.96   32.77

Based upon Andrei's continuous chatter about coordinates, we assumed that these were, in fact, coordinates.

Lonnie looked up a list of cities sorted by latitude. After a little research and guessing of our own, we deciphered them as the latitudes of Moscow, Havana, Tampa and Dallas.

Seemingly these coordinates led us through the assassination route. Just as many people had surmised, the KGB contracted with Santo Trafficante to carry out the deed. Who knows the full extent of what Trafficante got in return for murdering a US President? Maybe the undying loyalty of the KGB? I think we just laid the blame for the assassination right onto Trafficante's front doorstep.

There were rumors floating around for years that the KGB was involved. It is a fact that Lee Harvey Oswald met with Russian officials at the Soviet Embassy in Mexico City about two months before the assassination.

He subsequently made several more trips to Havana and Mexico City. These trips were documented by the CIA as were Oswald's many statements concerning his allegiance to communism. So, yeah, Oswald, nut job that he was, might have been conspiring with the KGB. Maybe the KGB kept him around as a wildcard to work with them, but he went rogue.

Lonnie looked at me and commented, "So the heavy handed one gets killed over an assassination that took place forty-seven years ago?"

Sam said, "Maybe he did, but what if Vasili wanted to protect his son from something the Russians were cooking up? Based on that premise, maybe Andrei left erroneous or misleading information on the CD? Maybe Andrei knew his life was in danger? There's got to be something on the CD that points us to the source of the radiation sickness cases."

***

The three of us mulled over what we had just learned from Andrei's Case Studies CD as well as some theories and conjectures about possible KGB links to the Kennedy assassination coupled with Mafia links to the assassination.

This was getting complicated. I mean, if the Senate Committees and House Committees on every topic under the sun haven't proved anything by now, then how is a clam digger from Long Island going to come up with the answers?

Moving away from the Kennedy thing, I asked Sam, "What was all that radiation sickness stuff that Andrei went on about?"

"At last year's conference, he told me that he had treated a few cases of radiation sickness at the request of the Cuban Government. He did so at a top security medical clinic located outside of Guantanamo. He didn't know where the cases originated. The government put a tight lid on that information. All he knew was that they were treated near Guantanamo."

"Really! Radiation sickness in Cuba? That's odd. Isn't it, Sam?"

"Yes, it is. I've never heard of that before. I think Andrei was trying to tell me about the Guantanamo facility on the night he was killed. I wonder who will care for those patients since Andrei is now out of the picture?"

"Andrei definitely had a lot on his mind … radiation sickness, Jack Kennedy and a top security medical clinic all marinating in Stolichnaya."

Then there were the mysterious geographic coordinates that Andy once raved about. Sam was scrolling through the actual case studies of the dead workers. He looked up, "Hey check this out, each study has the same exact numeric entry without an explanation of what it points to."

"Really," I said. "Is it coordinates again like Andy babbled about?"

"Yes it looks like it could be. Here you go …

'22.66.845 N   83.47.92 W

We pulled out a nautical map that showed that the coordinates were pointing into the Mariel area – we were sitting right on them!

Cuban Exile

August 1962 - The United States of America

Wal-Mart opens for the first time in Rogers, Arkansas.

Marilyn Monroe dies at age 36 after overdosing on sleeping pills.

Cuba Releases over 1100 prisoners from the Bay of Pigs Invasion.

Rachel Carson releases 'Silent Spring'.

Beach Boys release 'Surfin Safari'.

Ringo Starr replaces Pete Best as Beatles' drummer.

US performs nuclear test at Nevada Test Site.

USSR performs nuclear test at Novaya Zemlya USSR.

US U-2 flight locates SAM launch pads in Cuba.

The New York Yankees are on the way to their seventh World Series in eight years...

Chapter 29

Over lunch, I asked Sam about the old bartender at the Mariel Marina Inn. I had an idea building inside of me. I was not exactly sure where it was going. "Sam, didn't you say that the old bartender 'knew everything about everything' that has gone on in Mariel?"

"Yeah, so?"

"So the bartender must be in tight with Cabrara's cowboys."

"Probably."

"So let's plant a piece of misinformation with the bartender and see if it circulates through the cops and back around to us."

"Okay, but what will that prove?"

"I'm not quite sure."

***

Later that afternoon the three of us sat in a booth in the Mariel Marina Inn. Our favorite bartender was on duty and gave us a big, friendly smile. I ordered a Heineken while my sidekicks had Cuba Libres. We huddled together – with our heads hunched forward forming a tight triangle. It looked as if we were about to discuss a matter of great secrecy. I kept glancing over my shoulder, ostensibly to be on the lookout for potential spies who might be lurking around.

For a few minutes we talked about sailing, boat maintenance, baseball and anything else that would come to our minds. Finally, Sam said to me, "I think I have an idea about where these radiation sickness cases are originating from."

I glanced over my shoulder. "Go on."

"Andy's case files indicated that the victims were all government employees of the Havana Park Service. As such, they probably were working in an area with strong chemicals -- the kind needed to maintain a park or a golf course, possibly a place where radioactive materials somehow got into the picture."

"I don't get it, radiation from a park?"

"Good question. My guess is that there was a radiation leak – as crazy as that sounds -- in one of the public parks. I think Andy figured this out."

Lonnie added, "We are closer to figuring out how Andrei got himself killed. Maybe we shouldn't be discussing this here. Our little rouse has tuned into an actual detective investigation."

Our octogenarian bartender was wiping off the bar and glancing at us. Lonnie got up to pay the bill and asked the bartender, "Are there any golf courses in the area? We would like to get a tee time for tomorrow morning."

The bartender gave us more information about golf in the area than you would find in a travel brochure. He went on and on about the different courses and their characteristics. It was hard to break away. He even offered to get us a tee time at a nearby course. Lonnie accepted.

Chapter 30

Later that afternoon, I tracked down Ernesto at the docks. He was getting the *Mariel Maiden* ready for that evening's 'booze cruise.' We leaned against the railing on the boat and talked as the crew loaded up on ice, beer, plenty of rum and all the other things needed for a memorable sail into the sunset. Something about Ernesto made me want to trust him... so I did.

He turned to me and said, "I've been following you ever since your arrest. Carla was very worried. Come with me. There is someone I would like you to meet."

We walked over to a nearby thatched roof sitting area and each of us took a seat. We soon were joined by a dark-haired woman who wore a wraparound sarong dress and a halter top. She was tall, leggy and confident and slid into her seat with a sultry look that was coated with an alluring smile. She gave Ernesto a kiss that I thought lasted a little too long. Then she looked over and smiled at me.

I was quite taken by Adriana when she was introduced by Ernesto. I was sure it was a reaction she had seen many times before. Adriana said to me, "You don't remember me, do you?"

I wanted to say, *"How would any man in the world not remember you?"* but I didn't. Instead I said, "I'm afraid to say that I don't. Have we met?"

"Only when I had my blonde hair on."

Cuban Exile

"Your blonde hair?" I settled in to a good long look at this woman. Now that I was accused of a memory failure, I felt as if I was entitled to an extended observation of her finer points – that were considerable. It was the most fun I had had since getting out of the Cuban jail.

Ernesto broke the trance I was falling into, "Adriana was trailing you at the Mariel Inn on the nights that you were out drinking with the Russian. She wore a blonde wig."

"Right! I knew that."

"She was just checking on your well being." Ernesto leaned over close to me and said, "Cabrara has a long reach in this area. Adriana will tell you more."

Earlier in the day I wrote down the coordinates that appeared in the case studies on Andy's CD. I showed them to Ernesto, who immediately recognized them as the outer edge of Parque Nacional La Guira, a national park where Ernesto and other guides began their eco-tours of Cuba's beautiful wetlands.

This is where he met the beautiful Adriana. The eco-tour turned into a whirlwind affair for the two of them. Over the last few months they had fallen in love and began starting a new life together...

The eco-tours were conducted by kayak and were a favorite of tourists in the Mariel region. The guests would kayak down through the back waters of the park following the flow of the river and then get picked up by a van and driven back to the starting point. The eco-tour van and a few trucks from the Havana Park Service were the only motorized vehicles allowed in the Mariel wetlands area.

But lately Ernesto had seen an unusual amount of vehicular traffic from secretive looking black SUVs with no identifiers on them. Something was up. The SUVs took a course headed toward the middle part of the park – the part that was not open to the public.

Maybe Andrei was right about the coordinates having something to do with radiation sickness?

After his explanation of the eco-tour, Ernesto handed me two tickets to the booze cruise -- stood and went back to his duties on the *Maiden*.

I remained alone with Adriana. I didn't know it yet but she was about to become my date for the sunset booze cruise. Ernesto was never completely sure if he was being followed or not so he kept a low profile in Mariel, including his liaisons with Adriana. Maybe it was I who was being tailed?

I started to ask her a question when she placed her forefinger on her lips. "We will talk later when the band starts to play and people are loosened up. I want you to board the boat with me smiling like you will be getting into my pants later. Treat me like your lover so we can stand close together and make eyes at each other." Now this is a job I can do!

After a short while, the band began playing as people entered the launch area holding their tickets. Adriana took my arm as we walked up the gangplank and stepped aboard. She found us two seats by the railing while I brought back two Cuba Libres from the bar. We toasted and kissed as the *Mariel Maiden* pushed off from the dock. Our romantic journey had begun.

Two drinks later, we were still playing love birds as we walked around to different areas of the boat.

Adriana held me close to her and said, "As you know, Ernesto is driven to find out what happened to his parents."

A tourist couple came over to us and asked if we would take a picture of them. Adriana complied and they posed with big smiles and a great view of the harbor.

We passed a large cruise ship and continued our way down the inlet towards the Straits. The couple drifted away from us and Adriana continued, "I work in the Records Management Division for the City of Havana. Ernesto asked me if I could gain access to records from the early seventies … records of political dissidents."

"Did you find anything helpful?"

"Yes, after using some old passwords and secure record searches, I located entries for Ernesto's family … the Ramos family."

"So what did the records say?"

"The records showed that his parents were shot while trying to escape from a detention facility."

"Well, at least he found out what happened to them."

"But there's more. According to what was shown, the 'attending police officer' was none other than Private Miquel Cabrara."

Chapter 31

The news that Ernesto's and Carla's parents might have been killed by Cabrara left me stunned. I stared at the harbor lights as the *Mariel Maiden* made its way on a northbound heading. The band was in full swing playing island music along with the requisite Jimmy Buffet selections.

The bartender, a good-looking black guy with braided hair and a pearl white necklace, was mixing drinks faster than was allowed by the laws of physics. He tossed bottles in the air and caught them behind his back while he got the mixers together. Astounding!

Adriana pulled me towards her and whispered to me, "Ernesto is obsessed with what he learned about his parents. He wants to kill Cabrara. Cabrara is a beast ... a horrible person and a person with great power. It will take a lot to bring down a person like that."

"Yeah, and there's a good chance Ernesto could wind up dead in the process. How exactly does he plan on pulling this off?"

"He has noticed that Cabrara has been making almost daily visits, in the black unmarked government cars, to the park interior. He is doing something that requires his direct attention on a frequent basis. Sometimes there is a little fat guy with him."

"So Ernesto is going to hit Cabrara in the National Park and then what, go back to the tour boat and continue to look for gardenias in the rain forest?"

"I was warned that you are a smart ass."

"Yeah, well a smart ass is one thing, but killing the Chief of Police is quite another." I wasn't sure exactly how much I should know about the portion of the plan that Adriana just described. I mean, I just finished up with a week or so of Cabrara's hospitality. I didn't want to go back to the concrete bunker with rusty water. Besides, I was getting used to wearing clean shirts again.

The thing is though, I was already involved. It became clear that Ernesto's curiosity concerning the recent government excursions in the restricted area ran in parallel with the research data that was found on Andy's CD.

Cabrara was more than likely involved in radioactive materials of some sort … and they were stashed in the National Park. The materials were responsible for the deaths of several park employees. Ernesto had no knowledge of what Cabrara was really doing. He was just filled with hatred over what he had done to his parents.

Adriana went on to tell me that Ernesto's plan was to hit Cabrara with a long range rifle deep inside the park and then get on one of the return vans with the tourists. He would then move on to the dock and start loading up for that evening's sunset cruise. Next, he would pull the boat out as normal with the band playing and the bartender pouring.

I asked Adriana. "And I am involved how?"

"You see that lifeboat tethered to our tour boat?" I looked over to the main lifeboat … a twenty-two foot Boston Whaler with a twenty-five horsepower outboard engine. "Yeah, I see it – very nice boat."

"Well, when the time comes, we're going to have an impromptu safety drill on that boat once darkness begins to fall and we are somewhere out there in the Straits."

"Well, that's always a good practice. You do know that our sailboat cannot leave the dock?"

"Yes I do. The sailboat has nothing to do with this. We need you to talk to Carla. Ask if we can use one of her go-fast loaner boats to rescue us on the lifeboat and take us to Key West.

That little Boston Whaler will never make it through heavy seas out in the Straits. Ernesto can sneak away from the tour boat into the dark with the lifeboat, but we need a boat that can handle rough seas and get us to Key West."

"So we're going to need a bigger boat?"

"Yes, we are." Adriana totally missed my wisecrack.

"Is Carla aware of all of this? Does she know she may become involved in a conspiracy to commit murder?"

"Yes, Ernesto has told her everything. Carla has such faith in you. You're Johnny Donohue. You can do anything on the water. We need your help ... please. Navigate us through the Straits. Find a boat somehow that will get us safely out of Cuba."

"Okay, let me make sure I understand this. You want me to participate in hijacking the lifeboat that is used in fleeing the scene of the murder of the Chief of Police?"

"Yes, I guess I do."

"Well, forget it, Baby. We'll all wind up in a radioactive landfill until our skin glows. Sorry, Adriana, but this plan has disaster written all over it."

"Johnny, I am in love with Ernesto. We both want to get to the States – clear his name, reunite with his sister and live together like normal people."

"Adriana, that all makes for a beautiful story … except for the part where we all wind up in a Cuban prison."

I just couldn't believe that I was even listening to a conspiracy to commit the murder of a cop in a foreign country … even though I warned against it.

Still, I was treading in dangerous waters. I would need a detailed conversation with Lonnie about this whole thing.

The booze cruise had another hour left to go. We were out of the channel and into the Straits. I looked out upon a black sea and thought … *A little Boston Whaler with four people on board would struggle badly against this weather.*

I ordered another round of drinks as we headed back into Mariel. *What the hell did I get myself into?*

Chapter 32

The next morning Lonnie, Sam and I headed for the golf course. We checked in with the starter, rented three bags of clubs and took some practice swings.

I looked around the area a few times before I noticed our old friend, Luis Ramirez, of the Security Police sitting in his car at the end of the parking lot. There's just something about us that keeps drawing the attention of the Security creeps.

So, at least we knew that the bartender was reporting what he saw to Ramirez and his merry men ... no big surprise there. We continued through the golf charade for nine holes and then went back to the boat.

It was time for Sam to pack up and head to Tampa. His services were in demand. By nature of the agreement we signed with Cabrara, Lonnie and I were to stay put while Pavnara's murder investigation was going on.

I made a copy of Andrei's CD and loaded it onto my secure laptop. Sam took charge of the original. I also gave Sam and Lonnie the short version of Ernesto's escape plan. They listened in silence, each absorbing what they heard. "Ok", said Sam, "I am not getting involved in this. I am not risking my career over some cockamamie scheme to kill someone."

Lonnie grunted and then got up and helped Sam into a waiting taxi. When he came back into the cabin, I opened two Heinekens and stared up at the bulkhead.

Cuban Exile

Lonnie said to me, "Tell me you're not getting involved in this Ernesto thing."

"I'm not getting involved in this Ernesto thing."

"Then why do you look like you're getting involved in this Ernesto thing?"

"Well, it is Carla's brother and …"

Lonnie cut me off, "So you *are* getting involved in this Ernesto thing."

"Well," …

another cut-off, "Then count me out, okay? I am just going to quietly wait here until Cabrara cuts me loose. Then I am quietly sailing back to Key West … no siblings, no police, no funky bartender and most of all, no Cuban jail! You got that, Johnny? I am sailing to the good old USA. You know, the first amendment, baseball, cable TV."

"Yeah, I got it. I got it."

***

Lonnie, of course, was right. For all the smiling and pandering that politicians live by, Cuban civil rights had a long way to go. The little fat dumbo that represented the Security Police focused on crimes such as espionage, sabotage, and offenses against the state.

Yeah, offenses against the state. That's probably what Carla's parents were guilty of. That's what might have gotten Andrei killed. Maybe he was getting too used to covering up offenses against the state by way of dead bodies from the National Park.

I sipped my beer, laid on the bench and contemplated our situation. We were being tailed by the Cuban Security Police after being held for over a week by the Chief of Police. We had a dead Russian who spoke Stolichnaya, radioactive material floating around somewhere and who knows how many dead park employees. As a sidetrack we found out that KGB Admirals plotted to kill JFK by way of gangster Santo Trafficante.

Oh yeah, and off to the side we have Carla's brother planning not just any old murder but a murder of the Chief of Police. I reviewed my list of items with Lonnie who said, "Don't forget that we are sitting on a two hundred thousand dollar sailboat which is chained to the dock."

"Right."

"Johnny, we don't have to get involved with Ernesto but there is something that we need to act upon right away and I do mean right away."

"I know exactly what you're getting to. If we don't do something now, other people may die of radiation sickness."

"Ok, what can we do to stop Cabrara? He's got to be masterminding this whole thing?"

"We need help."

Chapter 33

We decided to contact the Swiss Embassy and get hold of one of those USINT Havana guys. It took more than an hour to find the right INT guy. This, in spite of the fact that I used my best charm and warmest wishes to the Swiss administrative staff who transferred me from one bureaucrat to another.

I didn't make any jokes about Switzerland and emphasized my love of chocolate and red suspenders.

What I did do was use my connection to Doctors Without Borders to gain access to someone who was trying to help. Lonnie and I were listed on the Mariel entry documentation as volunteers for the recent medical conference. We were granted an appointment for the next day with a Doctors Without Borders member, and embassy official, Mr. Justin Elder. Elder, an American, was in charge of writing up details of the last conference while planning the next one.

I was hoping to get a real Swiss guy, but no luck there. Lonnie and I spent the evening on the boat putting together the information we had acquired. Hopefully, this guy, Elder, would quickly recognize the gravity of the situation and move in on Cabrara. I would love to see that mother get nailed.

***

We arrived at the embassy promptly at 1 PM the next day and were led to Elder's office. At this point, we had decided to forgo any attempts of playing spy. We were not ostentatious in our arrival nor were we overly secretive. Lonnie and I arrived and departed separately using different entrances.

Elder was a forty-something serious heads-down worker with a no-nonsense air about him. He took out the notes he made yesterday and began. "Mr. Turner, you are an ex-marine and retired policeman?"

"Yes, that's right."

"And Mr. Donohue, you are …?" This question always confused me.

"I am a retired clam digger from Long Island." Elder was not amused but continued on. Lonnie gave me a look that said, *shut up, you asshole*.

We got the preliminaries taken care of in a hurry and then slipped into a long and detailed discussion of what had happened to us since we left Key West. It seemed like a hundred years ago.

After about an hour and a half, Elder stepped out and had his assistant bring in some coffee. We waited by ourselves for awhile before Elder came back in followed by an INT person whose security badge read Jack Dreersom. Dreersom introduced himself as an official of the International Atomic Energy Agency.

The IAEA, according to Dreersom, works for the safe, secure and peaceful uses of nuclear energy. Its key activities support international peace and security as well as the world's social, economic and environmental development. It sounded like a handful.

Cuban Exile

The IAEA acts as the world's nuclear inspector, performing a huge role in global efforts to stop the spread of nuclear weapons.

Dreersom was exactly what we needed right now! Lonnie and I shook hands vigorously with him. As it turned out, he was a real Swiss guy – no suspenders but still, the accent was clearly Swiss.

Dreersom verified what we already knew -- that the USINT Section of the Swiss Embassy in Havana represented US interests in Cuba. As such, it was staffed mainly by US Foreign Service personnel. So Americans, attached to the Embassy, moved around Cuba in a restricted but open manner.

The four of us sat in the office drinking coffee and comparing notes. I brought a copy of Andrei's CD. The CD was the key to so much in this discussion.

Lonnie led them through the different sections of the CD and stopped at the case studies of the dead park workers. Dreersom and Elder read these in silence and made some notes.

They asked to excuse themselves and more coffee arrived. When they returned, Dreersom laid a bombshell on us. "Gentlemen, we here at the IAEA have been suspicious for sometime now concerning the activities of Chief Cabrara and Security Officer Luis Ramirez. We think they are running a black market on nuclear materials – selling to third world countries … North Korea, Venezuela, the list goes on. Somewhere along the way the storage facility he is using has developed the equivalent of a nuclear leak. This is an extremely dangerous situation."

Dreersom went on to say that the CD gives the IAEA enough clout to approach the United Nations.

The UN could put diplomatic pressure on Cuba to cease and desist this criminal activity at once.

The IAEA could then close the damaged nuclear storage facility and bring to justice those involved. That's the theory anyway.

Having all this happen in a concise and orderly fashion is another thing. Meanwhile, people are dying of radiation sickness.

On a less dramatic note, Lonnie and I, along with *Epithelia,* were in custody until Cabrara decided otherwise. I, for one, had about enough of that. The US INT people were aware of that but there was little they could do about it. Cabrara was hiding behind his 'ongoing murder investigation' blanket so Lonnie and I were stuck.

As if that weren't enough, the whole Ernesto thing was looming out there looking like a very ugly baby. I hadn't mentioned Ernesto to the embassy people ... yet.

After about four hours in the embassy office, we agreed to meet up the next morning at 10 AM and continue whatever it was that we were doing.

This was getting complicated for a clam digger. I wished it would all go away. I wanted to be in the states – at a baseball game – with a lukewarm, overpriced beer.

As Elder ushered us out, he looked at me and said, "What was all that information about President Kennedy on the CD?"

"Well, I'm not exactly sure, but it looks like the Pavnaras are pointing the way to the assassination."

"Hmmm."

Cuban Exile

The United States of America October 1963

JFK Plans a Trip To Texas to Gain Support for the 1964 election.

The Washington-To-Moscow "Hot Line" Communications Link Opens. It Was Designed To Reduce the Risk Of Accidental War.

Liz Taylor stars in 'Cleopatra'.

The First 'Pink Panther' movie is released.

The US Continues to Build Troop Count in Viet Nam.

The Number One Song Is Jimmy Glimer and The Fireballs – 'Sugar Shack'.

President Kennedy's 'Ich bin ein Berliner' Speech Calls For the Free World to Stand Together Against Communism..

The Los Angeles Dodgers Sweep the World Series Taking Four Straight From The New York Yankees.

Chapter 34

We arrived back at the boat full of caffeine and full of questions. I know it's wishful thinking to want the IAEA people to say something like, "Good job guys. We'll take it from here. We'll arrest Cabrara and return your boat back. Thanks and good bye."

Clearly, that ain't going to happen. I mean, Dreersom and Elder were tracking down a black market in uranium or plutonium or whatever the hell it takes to set off a nuclear bomb! Then they're going before the United Nations.

I mixed up some dark rum and lime, Carla's favorite drink, and stretched out on the cabin bench. I said to Lonnie, "I think we have to let Ernesto know that he better back down off of his plan."

"You figured that out by yourself, Genius?"

"Pretty much, yeah."

"Brilliant."

"And what about our INT friends? Do we tell them about Ernesto? It's getting a little like 'Spy vs. Spy' around here. And another thing – Cabrara is undoubtedly involved in Andrei's murder. If he determines that we're playing footsie with the IAEA, we might be next."

"Let me ask you something, Johnny. What do you think, for us, is the quickest way off of Cuba?"

I didn't have to think very long before coming back with my answer. "Ernesto's lifeboat plan." Lonnie did not disagree. He answered his own question.

"Right, with Cabrara in a frenzy because his little black market scheme is going to hell and the IAEA people breathing down his neck, Cabrara is capable of anything. For God's sake, the guy used to torture people for living."

I thought, based on the statements we made when we were interrogated along with that two-way bartender, Cabrara had good reason to kill Andy.

Killing a few more people – like us and then suddenly pointing to us as the murderers might be exactly what he's up to right now. We needed to talk to Ernesto and we needed to put together our plans for getting off the island. I called Adriana and the four of us met at the thatched roof bar at the edge of the marina.

***

Over dinner Lonnie and I convinced Ernesto to abort his plan to kill Cabrara. We alluded to the fact that there were certain parties, based in the States, which were following Cabrara around and building a case against him.

We told Ernesto that his effort would only interfere with bringing Cabrara to justice. In addition, it would greatly jeopardize his own plan to escape with Adriana. The two of them needed to keep a low profile because Ernesto's life depended on it. If he gets caught by the Cuban Police, he's a dead man.

If Cabrara decides to frame Lonnie and me for Andy's murder, we could wind up just as dead.

Anyway you looked at it, we had to get the hell out of here and get out fast. This, we all agreed on.

We laid out the framework of our now mutual escape plan. Ernesto would run the eco-tour as usual. He then would prepare the tour boat for the sunset booze cruise.

Like a good first mate, he would check provisions and inspect all safety equipment. This was his opportunity to stash some necessities on board the lifeboat that might come in handy.

Lonnie and I would each board carrying tourist looking black backpacks. The packs would hold several flashlights, a hand-held Garmin GPS, a satellite phone, a diving knife, foul weather jackets and three thirty-eight caliber hand guns. These last items Lonnie managed to obtain from the local cops using American greenbacks as currency.

Ernesto carried a five-gallon jug of gasoline on board and strapped it down to the railing on the lifeboat ... just in case we might need it out there. Finally, we packed a hand-held marine radio.

As the booze cruise was on its way out to the Straits, the first mate would inform the captain of a problem with the suspension cable that secured one of the lifeboats. The captain of the tour boat would earlier have been provided with a special two hundred dollar bonus for ignoring any shenanigans that might go on surrounding the lifeboat or lack of it.

The other side of the plan depended entirely on Carla coming through with a boat big enough to handle four extra adults safely. We had to connect with Carla and her borrowed boat by way of a rendezvous point somewhere out there in the Florida Straits.

Cuban Exile

The four of us went over the plan several times – correcting small points as we came across them. Lonnie and I would come up with exact rendezvous coordinates – verify them with Ernesto and then transmit them to Carla. There was no need to pull up a nautical chart in the middle of a crowded bar. Who knows who might be watching?

We finished dinner and ordered a round of drinks. Ernesto sat back, pulled out a Cuban cigar and lit it ceremoniously; setting off a series of concentric smoke rings. He sipped his Cuba Libre and proceeded to tell us about his baseball career that showed such promise all those years ago.

When he played in high school, as Ernesto Ramos, he led his team in all offensive categories – batting average, home runs and runs batted in. He even played ball during his mandatory service to the state. Ramos was on his way to playing professional baseball in the Cuban minor league system. He completed two solid seasons and became a sought-after player.

When Ernesto's parents mysteriously disappeared, he became fearful for his own life and for the welfare of his sister, Carla. That is when he decided to escape to America. He knew he was good enough to play major league ball in the States but didn't know where to go or who to talk to.

He needed to survive. He needed money. That is how he very briefly got involved with a drug gang. Ernesto knew that was a dead end for any kind of life, so he got out of it. Unfortunately, there was a dead body lying around as a result of his involvement. He was wanted in connection with the killing of a dealer.

In those days that was ho-hum. Who cares? He

soon got hold of falsified records – driver's license, social security card, birth certificate through the help of his aunt. In the early 1970s, it was relatively easy to do this.

Ernesto went to a Florida State League walk-on open tryout session and was immediately signed by the League. He played two full seasons as a second baseman before badly injuring his knee in a violent slide by an opposing player. Ernesto never recovered from that injury and never played professional ball again.

We talked baseball for awhile before going our separate ways. We agreed to move forward quickly on our plan and to meet at another, more remote, restaurant the following night. After that we were headed to Key West.

Lonnie and I went back to the boat and agreed to treat the night like an overnight trip on the Gulf – meaning someone was on watch at all times through the night – only this watch was for our dockside security.

Years ago, an old salt at a marina told me to keep a spray can of wasp repellant aboard the boat. If someone on the boat was about to do you harm, spray him in the face with this stuff. It is a non-lethal method of getting someone away from you in a hurry.

They will be suffering from coughing, sneezing and burning eyes – all of which are temporary but give you time to get things under control. That night I stood my watch with a can of wasp spray nearby.

About 3 AM I felt the boat list gently towards the dock. A stranger in a black hoodie came on board and was about to climb down the companionway ladder. I blasted him in the face with the spray can and he jumped back onto the pier and started running, screaming and rubbing his eyes, I didn't think we would see him again. I guess he'll report back to Cabrara -- Mission not accomplished!

Lonnie woke up and I told him what had happened. "You know," he said. "Let's ask the IAEA people to get all four us out of here. That way we avoid any midnight offshore rendezvous and we get home dry."

"A nice thought but we better prepare for the escape plan because getting help from the government is a long shot at best."

Later that morning, we double checked our packs to make sure we had the items we would need for the lifeboat escape. We pulled up a nautical chart on my laptop and chose the critical rendezvous point. We checked it and then checked it again. We were ready to go.

Chapter 35

At 10 AM, Lonnie and I headed over to the Swiss Embassy to meet up with our IAEA contacts. They verified what we had previously discussed concerning Cabrara's activities. At that point the conversation abruptly ended.

This was my cue to ask about safe passage out of Cuba. I did not mention Ernesto by name – only that we needed help for ourselves and two others in leaving Cuba. We were treading on thin ice between Cabrara and the IAEA.

If the INT people could get the four of us out of Cuba, there would be no need for an escape plan at all.

I broached the topic of our desire to get out of Cuba. I flat out asked Jack Dreersom of the IAEA to arrange a one-way flight for four to Key West. He refused. "We cannot violate any Cuban laws, Mr. Donohue. Otherwise, our status here will become persona non grata."

"You know Cabrara and those mother fuckers want to charge us with murder. Do you know what that means? It means a Cuban jail cell for us!"

"I cannot help violate any Cuban laws, Mr. Donohue."

"Yeah, yeah, yeah. Persona non whatever the hell it is -- you take all the information we gave you and then you throw us back onto the streets?"

"Mr. Donohue our mission is to stop wayward nations from obtaining fissionable materials. That mission supersedes the needs of four people who want to leave the country. Surely you can understand that?" I did but I was hoping to find an easy way off of the island.

I mean, it's not like Humphrey Bogart and Ingrid Bergman but it was all I had. I told him this was not going to be the beginning of a long and beautiful friendship. He ignored me. Bastard. Maybe he never saw Casablanca. We had to go with plan B.

Dreersom gave us the bum's rush out the door -- a complete reversal of the treatment we received the day before. I didn't even have time to make wisecracks about the Swiss.

***

We spent the rest of the day taking care of the boat. I wasn't sure whether Sam would ever see her again. I'm sure the Cuban Police would be the new owner but it would probably be in the slip at the marina for some time.

We decided to leave the boat and get a hotel room for the night – our last night in Cuba. I didn't want to meet up with the wasp spray guy again. We had our backpacks ready to go so we headed out separately to a small local hotel and checked in.

We had nothing to do but wait for evening to roll around and finalize things with Ernesto. With his approval, we would transmit the rendezvous coordinates to Carla and she would return the make and model of the rescue boat. The rendezvous coordinates as we had them were …

23° 53' 19 N   81° 46' 58 W …

Using an approximate speed of ten knots, this would put us out in the Straits about three hours north of Mariel. That is, provided we had ample horsepower and the weather cooperated.

There was one task that we would tend to at cocktail hour. This involved Lonnie and I in a bit of subterfuge by way of our favorite bartender at the Mariana Marina Inn – back where this whole thing started.

We sat hunched over the bar quietly discussing plans for a 7 PM flight to Miami the following night. If my hunch was right, Cabrara would get this news with time enough to post some extra security at the Havana Airport – far away from where we would be headed. That ought to keep the Cuban Security Police busy for awhile

Adriana and Ernesto showed up for dinner about 7 PM. We reviewed our plan again; this time including the rendezvous coordinates. Carla connected with Ernesto earlier in the day. The rescue craft would be a sixty-five-foot Bayliner with dual three-hundred horsepower outboard engines. The hull would be navy blue making it a little more difficult to see at night. The vessel name was *Blue Monday*.

We talked a little more, finished dinner and headed back to our respective locations – for the last time. Tomorrow night would be a busy night. I must admit, I was a little afraid to be out in the Straits at night, with no running lights, in a small boat. But I was more afraid of going back to jail in Cuba. I thought to myself, *If I ever get out of this one alive, I'm never going to leave the United States again.*

Chapter 36

The booze cruise was on time for its usual 6 PM departure. Lonnie, Adriana and I boarded about 5:45 or so. I looked around but didn't see Ernesto. He was probably on shore side taking care of some last minute details. He finally showed up looking sweaty and disheveled, right as the *Mariel Maiden* was backing out from the dock. He too had a backpack that he wore as he greeted guests with his smile.

Typically, the tour boat cruise lasted until shortly after 8 PM. If all went well, they wouldn't miss us until the final head count. By that time we would be well out to sea.

The booze cruise did not disappoint. After about thirty minutes into it, people were on their second or third drink. The thirty-somethings were the noisiest.

They did shots of Tequila while toasting the upcoming sunset. They took endless cell phone pictures and laughed through every one of them. The weather was beautiful, the drinks were flowing, the band was playing – life was good.

About ten miles off shore, when First Mate Ernesto Clemente made his announcement about a mandatory lifeboat drill, hardly anyone noticed. People were all elbowing for a slot at the bar or a seat on the bulkhead. The more festive guests were dancing in the middle of the deck area.

Ernesto slipped over the side and released the cable from the lifeboat. He lowered it away as we all passed him our backpacks. Each of us boarded the lifeboat with caution. The outboard engine started right up and we were off! Ernesto took the wheel with his backpack resting on deck squeezed between his knees. Adriana sat closely beside him with her hand on his knee. Lonnie and I were in the small stern seats.

We were about to leave Cuban territorial waters as we made our way north approaching Cuba's twelve-mile limit. Territorial Waters, loosely known as the Law of the Sea, is a belt of waterways defined by the coastline that traverses a given nation.

These waters may extend out as far as twelve nautical miles from a coastal state. Territorial Waters are regarded as the sovereign territory of a given coastal state. To make things a little friendlier though, foreign ships are allowed innocent passage.

The rest of the waterways – international waterways -- are theoretically a free-for-all. I'm not sure what exactly happens to stolen boats cruising around with a cache of weapons and no lights but I didn't think it was good.

We made less than ten knots of speed as the wind turned against us and blew directly from the northwest. Lonnie and I were taking on water in the face. We struggled to put on foul weather jackets.

According to our position and speed, we had about thirty nautical miles to go – approximately three hours to the rendezvous point. Darkness was on its way so we all donned orange life vests. They were the cheap, bulky kind that you find on tourist boats all over the world.

The final glimmers of sunset were blinding if you dared to turn your eyes to the west. In the distance cargo ships crawled their way east and west through the straits. They were settling in for a long night at sea.

Ernesto reached into his backpack and pulled out a six-foot retractable radio antenna. He extended it and quickly fixed it to the binnacle railing. Next he pulled out a sophisticated long range radio and connected to the antenna.

This is not something we had talked about during our planning sessions. I poked Ernesto in the back. When he turned his head towards me I asked him, "Hey, what are you doing? Someone can pick us up on a scanner. We never talked about a long range radio."

"Well, we're going to talk about it now. I need to monitor some radio traffic. I want to know if people are looking for us."

With that, Lonnie joined in the conversation. He glared at Ernesto, "You took out Cabrara, didn't you – back there in the National Park?"

"I had my chance and I took it. Cabrara killed my mother and father."

"Yeah and now every boat in the Cuban Police and Cuban Navy will be looking for us! Shut that goddamned radio off before I stick it down your throat."

While this friendly little dialogue went on, a police broadcast came across the scanner indicating that a Cuban Policeman had been killed outside of the National Park near Mariel. It was believed that the suspects escaped by boat. Adriana took the radio from Ernesto, turned it off and put it back in his pack.

I was seething at Ernesto. "Great move, asshole. Why don't you just broadcast our position to all boats in the area -- or better still, throw up a flare so that they can find us even easier. I can't believe you shot the Chief of Police. We talked about this asshole –

remember? Now we're open season for any boat that floats by."

We were approaching two hours to the rendezvous position. The weather was worsening but not intolerable. The wind increased to about twenty knots. Waves broke over the gunwale and ran out the scuppers in the stern of the boat. Seas looked to be from three to five feet high with the occasional seven-footer coming around. I felt as if I could strangle Ernesto to death right there on the spot. My anger was running wild.

The two of us were trading insults and threats when Lonnie announced, "Oh boys, I think we have company. Boat traffic off the stern. Ernesto what else do you have in that bag?"

He went into his pack and pulled out one of those rifles that are assembled from components and loaded quickly. Lonnie grabbed the barrel and stock. He put the weapon together and loaded it with a clip. He did not return it to Ernesto but instead put it inside a locker on the starboard side of the boat.

Lonnie handed me a loaded thirty-eight caliber pistol and I stuffed it inside my waistband in the small of my back. I pulled my jacket over it and hoped I would not have to use it. Lonnie did the same with his thirty-eight. He also held the rifle in his lap. Ernesto would get nothing.

The boat off of the stern was gaining on us in spite of the heavy seas. I couldn't see the lettering but my hunch said Cuban Police. If Ernesto had killed Cabrara, the police would have access to any boat they wanted and any personnel they needed. It was going to take a miracle to get us out of this one alive!

The Cuban Police boat turned on a big searchlight and began sweeping the area. They must have seen us at the time but who knows? I pulled out the satellite phone and dialed Carla. It took almost twenty seconds to connect but I managed to give her our current location.

She had problems understanding me so I repeated my message and waited for her reply. Just when she seemed to be receiving it the connection died. Water was ankle deep on the deck. The wind and rain, combined with the engine noise, made it almost impossible to communicate.

Before I could complete the call, the Cubans had spotted us and were moving to a position on our port side. One of them had a megaphone in hand, demanding us to heave to. He was demanding in Spanish so I threw up my hands as if I didn't understand.

I looked over at Ernesto and said, "Here, take the marine radio and issue a 'May Day'. Do it in English. Then try Carla again on the satellite phone. Tell her to issue her own 'May Day' from her marine radio. The US Coast Guard has got to be somewhere around here. See if she was able to receive our last position."

Chapter 37

Two armed Cuban Police made menacing gestures towards us with their machine guns at the ready. They were in a serious go-fast drug interdiction boat. We were no match for these guys. They stayed close to our port side as the helmsman bumped our hull a few times.

These guys were pissed. They were just a few feet away from us as they continued with their ramming act. I was desperately trying to buy some time by waving them off; hoping that one of our messages would get through. All the while, the weather was deteriorating. A steady rain was now coming down and visibility had dropped to a hundred yards or so.

Even in this weather, I recognized the Cuban Boat as a cutter boat. It is a rigid-hulled inflatable with a fixed canopy that houses a small control room. When the plastic drop-down windshields are deployed it is pretty well protected from the elements.

The cutter is in service with the US Coast Guard, the Cuban Maritime Police and other marine authorities throughout the world. Its twenty-five foot length can accommodate four crewmen comfortably – five or six if you're in need. It is usually powered by an inboard/outboard diesel engine with over three hundred horsepower. Quite a difference from a twenty-five horsepower outboard. We were screwed!

Ernesto kept trying these ridiculous evasive tactics. A ten year old could have done a better job. I yelled over to him "Put it in neutral and let them board."

Lonnie added, "Do whatever they say so we don't get shot to death out here." Ernesto did as he was told without saying a word.

The Cuban boat had a crew of two uniformed police spread across the gunwales in a firing position. They also had an officer inside the small, covered, control area. The Cutter brought itself parallel to our Whaler. Seas were getting worse as the two boats bobbed up and down together – bouncing against each other: sometimes the boats were in sync and sometimes not.

One of the Cubans threw a grappling hook over our bulkhead. Then he pulled us in close and tied the line tightly to a cleat on his boat. We were now abreast of each other. Waves were breaking over both boats as the seas continued to build. I was still killing time – fooling with lines – doing whatever I could to slow things down. Carla had to be approaching but she would be suffering from the same weather conditions that we were dealing with.

One of the Cubans made a hands up motion to all of us. Then he yelled something in Spanish that I also think was also a hands up thing. Now, a hands up directive is fine and dandy when you are holding up a bank on the mainland, but out here in heavy weather it was impossible to follow. You needed to hang on to anything that would keep you in the boat.

This was one of those times when I wished I had taken Spanish in high school. The Cubans were yelling at us, yelling at each other and seemingly yelling at the weather conditions. I put my hands up for a moment but quickly got knocked down onto the deck. I looked at the Cubans with a *What did you expect* face. They could take their hands up directive and stick it! Finally, Ernesto told them, in Spanish, that no one in their right mind could be hands up on this boat.

One Cuban looked at Ernesto's backpack and demanded that he pass it over to the police boat. Ernesto picked it up and pushed it towards the bow. As the guard reached down to grab it, a seven-foot wave came crashing against the boats. The Cuban lost his footing, fell and smashed his forehead against the edge of our lifeboat before tumbling into the water.

We all stood frozen, staring down at the guy who went overboard. The water around his head soon turned a distinctive red color that morphed into pink. He had a huge gash across his forehead. He was bleeding profusely – blood dripping down his face and into his mouth; his eyeballs staring up in disbelief.

In a few seconds, Adriana grasped the urgency of the situation. She leaned over the bulkhead, grabbed onto the man's life vest and pulled him up and out of the water. Now we had a wounded Cuban Policeman aboard our boat!

The other Cuban guard went back to yelling again. Adriana ignored him. She didn't let on that she spoke Spanish. She pulled a first aid kit out of her backpack and found some bandages. The injured Cuban continued to bleed badly. Adriana wrapped an ace bandage around his head but blood quickly seeped through. This guy needed help beyond that which a first aid kit could provide.

The remaining Cuban guard side-stepped his way to the control room, all the while keeping his eyes on us. The officer in the control room gave some kind of order that didn't sound good at all. Ernesto yelled out, "They are going to kill us."

With that, the officer at the control stepped out and revealed himself. It was Cabrara! That miserable son of a bitch was alive. He had a forty-five caliber hand gun pointed in my direction. The Police boat bobbed up and down with the waves. Any shooting would have been erratic at best but I couldn't just stand there and hope for the best.

I looked at Lonnie and we both leaped into the Police Boat. Lonnie tackled the guard down to the deck and beat him about the head until he seemed to have lost conscientiousness. In the process, Lonnie took a few punches to the body. He was pressing on his rib with one hand -- doubled over in pain while holding onto the railing with the other. It appeared that he had suffered a broken rib.

I signaled Ernesto to help Lonnie back onto the lifeboat and then to remove the grappling hook. The hook was only complicating things in the heavy weather. Our boats could easily get swamped if they remained tied together. Besides, the best way to get Lonnie some medical attention would be if Carla found us and we weren't encumbered by pulling along another boat. Ernesto took control of the lifeboat and slowly moved it away from the Police boat.

I was on my own with Cabrara. At his direction, I moved to the stern of the boat. He kept the pistol aimed at me while glancing towards the bow to steer the boat. Without warning, Cabrara gunned the powerful engines and knocked me backwards into the transom and then over the side.

Suddenly, I was in the water at night with a heavy sea ... and I was alone!

Chapter 38

I hit the water with my mouth wide open out of surprise and out of shock. As a result, I had swallowed a lot of salt water and was choking badly and spitting out water. I got very cold – very fast. *Try not to panic.* I thought. Well who the hell wouldn't panic in this situation?

Cabrara and his Police boat were in sight but of no use to me. He was moving away from me towards the lifeboat. I guess he expected me to drown. Cabrara was a ruthless bastard. He made no attempt to retrieve his own wounded, one of whom was aboard the lifeboat and the other missing in action.

I floated around in the Straits for what seemed like forever. I thought about sharks. I thought about my life and all the mistakes that I had made. I wondered what the survival time was in water with a temperature of seventy degrees. I wondered if this was my last day on Earth.

I leaned my head back onto the neck of the orange life jacket and looked up into the night sky. This allowed for a small amount of rest while treading water. I moved along with the current and offered no resistance to the waves. I simply rode up and down with them hoping someone would find me.

I was getting colder and couldn't help but think about the possibility of hypothermia. Even on a relatively warm day, boaters who have capsized and have been in the water for a prolonged period of time have come down with hypothermia. It simply means that your core body temperature drops below ninety-five degrees. In severe hypothermia, core body temperature can drop to eighty degrees or lower. Movements become slow and labored. Even raising up your arm becomes a chore. That's when organs start to shutdown and the end is near.

I was getting sluggish and tired. I was losing strength and had to fight hard to keep afloat. That was when I saw the searchlight of an approaching vessel.

The light described an arc of about one hundred eighty degrees as the boat moved towards me. I waved and yelled like a high school cheerleader. In the distance it seemed to be the sixty-five footer that Carla had promised. She found me!

Carla's boat slowed to a crawl as I slowly moved to the stern side swim platform. I was freezing and exhausted as I reached the swim ladder. Someone's hand grasped onto mine and helped to pull me up onto the platform. To my astonishment, DeeDee was aboard and had taken my full soaking wet body and dragged it up on top of her and onto the swim platform. We simply had to stop meeting like this.

DeeDee wiggled herself out from underneath me and wrapped me up in a blanket. Then she smothered me with her own body in an attempt to stop the intense shivering that I was going through.

Her warm body was the last I remembered of that night.

***

When I finally came around to a normal state of mind, I was lying in a hospital bed at the Lower Keys Medical Center. The nurse told me that I had been there for the last thirty-six hours.

I had one of those idiotic hospital gowns on. Basically, I was in for observation, to make sure that none of my internal organs hadn't floated away into the Straits.

Lonnie was one bed away in the same room. He had a cracked rib and was on some serious pain killers. The both of us would be resting for a few days. Carla came to visit us and smuggled in two Heinekens. She told the story of what had happened the night they pulled me out of the water.

It seems that the Coast Guard and Carla arrived at our rendezvous at approximately the same time. The Coast Guard came in two separate boats. They boxed in Cabrara on the port and starboard sides while Carla blocked him from escaping off of his stern. She brought the bow of the sixty-five-footer right up to Cabrara's stern and was about to ram him when DeeDee spotted me in the water.

She pulled me out as Carla called the Coast Guard to alert them of her intention to proceed to Key West with an injured crewman aboard.

Somehow, all of the boats, from the small lifeboat to the imposing Coast Guard vessels, made their way back to Key West. The Coast Guard boarded Cabrara's Police boat and placed him under arrest. It must have been quite a flotilla. I asked Carla, "How did DeeDee get involved?"

"Well, Sam sent her down in case you guys were going to sail his boat back from Cuba. When we learned that it was confiscated, she just decided to stay for awhile. I put her up in one of my marina boats and we became fast friends. She was great out there when all the trouble began."

"Yeah, she saved my life. You just never know about people."

In the days that followed, Lonnie and I were both interviewed by the US Coast Guard, the Key West Criminal Investigations Division and the INT people. Oh yeah, the FBI as well. These groups handled such things as murder at sea, attempted murder at sea, assaulting an officer of the US Coast and a few others that I had lost track of.

As if that wasn't enough, we also reacquainted ourselves with Mr. Jack Dreersom of the International Atomic Energy Agency. The IAEA was there to present evidence to the United Nations of illegal trafficking of nuclear materials. We were expected to help with that effort. I told Dreersom to buzz off. He could have gotten us passage out of Cuba but he didn't want to violate any local laws. As a result I was almost lost at sea – well to hell with you Dreersom.

My old buddy, Chief of Police Miquel Cabrara, was held without bail in the Key West lock up. To begin with, he was charged with attempted murder at sea. More importantly, he was charged with participating in a criminal conspiracy to illegally transport fissionable materials. They were going to throw the key away on this prick.

Chapter 39

Once we were out of the hospital, Lonnie and I spent over several days being grilled by all of the pertinent government organizations. The Key West Police were generous enough to lend us an interview room. They even gave me the cipher lock combination to get in and out of the room. I told my story over and over from Andrei Pavnara to landing in the Florida Straits in a life jacket.

One afternoon I had some dead time in between interviews. I walked down the hall of the police station to get some coffee. I passed by two interview rooms and stopped dead at a third. I couldn't believe my eyes.

Cabrara was sitting at a table in the room. This time he was wearing orange. I used my code, opened the door and went in.

I set the automatic lock behind me. Cabrara started to say something when I dragged him out of his chair by the collar of his prison outfit.

I punched him hard in the face and then pounded his stomach with my fist. He doubled over. I took the back of my elbow and bashed it hard into his nose. Blood started to stream down his face. I knocked him to the floor and knelt down beside him with my hands on his throat. I banged his head on the concrete floor until he lay there motionless.

All of this happened within the space of a minute or so. I stood up, unlocked the door and continued down the hall for my coffee. I returned innocently and awaited my next interview. Nobody tries to kill Johnny Donohue and gets away with it!

Cuban Exile

After more time had passed, the scattered pieces of my life started to come together. I went shopping with Carla and DeeDee and bought myself three or four new jackets. These I let settle in as the background pieces for my new wardrobe.

Carla turned out to be quite the fashion consultant – that is for a woman who mostly wore halter tops and khakis. DeeDee picked out some Columbia sailing shirts to go along with new boat shoes.

The new wardrobe landed in Carla's marina apartment as we had been living together ever since I got out of the hospital. I was in no particular hurry to leave Key West. Unlike Lonnie, who had a relationship to get back to, I was pretty much a free bird.

I got back to being involved in my marina software business which my partner kept going while I was in Cuba bringing down international criminals and solving the JFK assassination mystery.

I watched from a distance as Carla and her brother reunited. The years that they spent apart seemed to melt away as they sat in Carla's kitchen – laughing – crying -- each telling the story of their lives.

Ernesto and I were back to being friends. We talked about his attempt at killing Cabrara and how it almost got everyone else killed. We managed to get by that and never mentioned it again. It's tough to fault a guy for avenging his parent's killers while being robbed of a free man's life.

As it tuned out Adriana knew a Cuban couple in Key West who had a ten year old son. The kid was crazy about baseball. One day Ernesto and I took him up to Miami to see the Marlins play.

Ernesto told the boy of his baseball career and what it meant to him. The kid was in awe. Ernesto was proud and happy. He showed his young fan some of the finer points of the game while filling him up with hot dogs.

A few days after the Marlin's game Ernesto got himself a job coaching baseball at a private school in the area. His time in professional ball was short but apparently enough to give him a new start all these years later. He and Adriana had finally settled into the life they had dreamed about back in Cuba.

***

The big loose end in this whole adventure was *Epithelia.* It still sat there in the marina at Mariel chained to the dock. Sam wanted his boat back but I wasn't volunteering to go and get it. He wound up having Doctors Without Borders influence the powers that be to release the boat into their custody. They then contracted with a licensed captain to deliver the boat to Key West.

When *Epithelia* arrived it was cause for yet another dock party. People came by to see the boat that played such a big part of our Cuban adventure. A Key

West police officer, Carleton Briggs, came by to join in the festivities. I knew him from all of my time being interviewed at the station. He was off duty so he grabbed a beer and came aboard.

Briggs and I chatted about this and that before he told me, "We had a prisoner beaten up pretty badly last week."

"Really?"

"Yeah, he wound up with a serious concussion. It put him in the hospital."

"So, how's he doing?" Briggs ignored my last question. I said, "How about another beer?"

"Johnny, do you know anything about this?" I waxed poetic for a moment saying, "You know, justice has a way of coming around every once in awhile and tying the score."

"So that's your answer? Justice is evening things out."

"Yeah, that's my answer. Maybe the guy was guilty -- guilty of something terrible – crimes against humanity – attempted murder. Maybe this was justice coming in the back door and dealing with it in the best way possible."

Briggs and I had another beer and gradually became friends. We never again spoke of the workings of justice or the misfortune of a certain prisoner.

***

To my surprise, Sam flew down to Key West and reacquainted himself with his sailboat. He announced to one and all that he was sailing her up to

Bradenton and welcomed all able-bodied seamen to share in this momentous adventure.

The able-bodied seamen who accepted this challenge were myself and DeeDee, although I always considered DeeDee much more than able-bodied. We went through our drill of preparing the boat for a trip of two hundred miles. It took us three full days to get ready. This time I had Sam do most of the work.

One afternoon, Sam and I sat down in the cabin of *Epithelia* and talked about the CD that Andrei had given him.

He looked at me. "I went over the CD again and I think we were right about JFK's assassination, but I also think there's more to it."

"Yeah, we're probably about as right as anyone who has looked at this thing."

"Well, the Russians built missile silos to hide their nukes underground. When the nuclear missiles were taken out, there were empty silos hanging around Cuba."

I interrupted Sam. "Yeah, so along comes the KGB and Trafficante. Trafficante, of course, already has a sophisticated smuggling operation going on.

"The KGB promises to let Trafficante expand his operation to include fissionable materials. These materials would be stored in the silos and be worth millions to rogue countries and terrorist organizations. In return Trafficante has to kill JFK."

"Right," said Sam, "but he never had to kill the president because Lee Harvey Oswald got in the way."

"Yes, but the empty silos were just sitting there – waiting to be used."

We continued on for awhile. Each agreeing with the other's comments. We concluded that, at some point, the Cuban Security Police and Fidel must have gotten wind of what was going on with the silos. As the years went by, they nurtured people like Cabrara to manage the day to day operations.

Things were running smoothly until Andrei found out about the dead park workers. Radiation leaks were discovered in the aging silos and Cabrara's world started to come apart … too bad. I hope he enjoys his time in jail. He and the IAEC will have lots to talk about.

Chapter 40

On the night before we left Key West, Sam and DeeDee, along with Carla and I had dinner aboard the *Blue Monday*, our rescue boat from the Cuba episode.

DeeDee played hostess and made a beautiful dinner of grilled cod fish which she served on a bed of brown rice. The rice was embellished with small bits of broccoli. It all went beautifully with a good California chardonnay. She was a continuing surprise to me.

I wasn't sure, at all, as to when I would be back to Key West. Carla and I kind of danced around that topic. After dinner the two of us climbed up topside leaving the cabin to Sam and DeeDee. We put our feet up on the cushions and took in the night air. We didn't say much – just our own silent good-byes.

***

Carla came walking down the dock in the early morning hours to see us off and to collect Sam's dock fee. She did her typical boat entry; gliding off of the bow and down into the cabin while holding her clip board. We held each other for awhile before she disappeared back over the railing and down the dock.

I started the engine while Sam and DeeDee handled the lines. As I moved the boat through the marina, I noticed a new tour boat tied to the dock. It had a big sign draped across the hull that read …

Cuban Exile

Ecology Tours of Cuba.

Sign Up Here ...

As for Cuba, I don't think I'll be visiting there anytime soon. The Cuba Libres are great but their prisons really need a lot of improvement.

I am an American. I have rights here. I have due process here. I have a judicial system here and I have freedom here.

I can petition the government and I can criticize the government and I can do so without fear of reprisals.

These rights must not only be preserved and treasured but enhanced and nurtured by future generations of Americans.

Each must understand the gifts they have been given. They should embrace these freedoms and act upon them lest they go undefended, unprotected and unchallenged. This is the legacy that Jack Kennedy left us. This is the legacy he believed in when he said ...

"... Ask not what your country can do for you.
Ask what you can do for your country..."

I passed the Key West Sea Buoy just after sun up and set a northerly course taking us up the coast of Florida. I was going home.

Sandy Mason

The End

Author's Note

The Cuban Missile Crisis of 1962 brought the planet closest than it has ever been to nuclear annihilation. President Kennedy, using pure strength and wisdom, averted that Crisis.

A lot has been written, good and bad, about Jack Kennedy and the Crisis and what he did and what he should have done. There's plenty of criticism to go around but the fact is we wouldn't have the luxury of this speculation had Kennedy not saved us.

Soviet Commander Vasili Alexandrovich Arkhipov also did his part to save the world. The passages in this book concerning Arkhipov and his actions during the Crisis are completely true.

The story of his son and the KGB are purely the product of my over-active imagination.

Several people have helped out in the creation of this book. Marc Fleege contributed his knowledge of Cuba as well as all things nautical.

Nothing is accomplished without good editors and I owe a tremendous debt to Rick Millilo, JoAnne Quent, Heather Nicoll and Adrian VanEss.

Finally, my eternal gratitude to Laura Lake for story line development. Her imagination and support keep me going.

Cuban Exile

Sandy Mason is a long time resident of Eastern Long Island and the West Coast of Florida. He is the author of the Johnny Donohue Adventures. His novels include …

Storm Damage

Man Overboard

Sailor Take Warning

Shoreline

Havana Moon

Silver Voyage

Cuban Exile

All books are available from Amazon.com in both printed and Kindle editions.

Visit Sandy at www.Sandy Mason.com
Email SandyMason2782@aol.com
Visit Sandy via Amazon at
https://www.amazon.com/author/sandymason

Sandy Mason

Cuban Exile

37946284R00103

Made in the USA
Middletown, DE
12 December 2016